Frankenclaus Presents

A Frankenclaus Christmas For Santa Claus

Introducing

Doctor-Franken-Jack-Claus
If My Animals Go I Go!

The Frankenclaus Family of Friends

Copyright © 2020

Frankenclaus LLC. All rights reserved.

Frankenclaus Presents

A *Frankenclaus* Christmas For Santa Claus

ISBN-13 eBook1: 978-1-64586-000-6

ISBN-13 Paperback: 978-1-64586-001-3

ISBN-13 Large Print 16pt Paperback: 978-1-64586-002-0

ISBN-13 Large Print 18pt Paperback: 978-1-64586-003-7

ISBN-13 Giant Print 20pt Paperback: 978-1-64586-004-4

ISBN-13 Giant Print 24pt Paperback: 978-1-64586-005-1

Scripture Verses from King James Version

Printed and bound in the United States of America.

First Printing August 2020

Frankenclaus LLC Press

Dedication

The Frankenclaus Christmas Book Series
is dedicated to God's very special kids.

We love them all. -FFF

For Those Who Are Born Different,
But Born Okay.
Were you born different?
If so, you are in the right place.
You can relax.
You're Okay.
Breathe.

The Ten Commandments
of
Christmas Clausdom

1. Thou shalt love Christmas with all thy heart.

2. Thou shalt honor Christmas with all thy soul.

3. Thou shalt serve Christmas with all thy strength.

4. Thou shalt support Christmas with all thy worldly possessions.

5. Thou shalt protect Christmas from all adversaries; foreign and domestic.

6. Thou shalt give a Nice List to each Claus descendent each December.

7. Thou shalt give a Naughty List to each Claus descendent each December.

8. Thou shalt give Nice gifts to Nice children on Christmas morning.

9. Thou shalt give Naughty gifts to Naughty children on Christmas morning.

10. Thou shalt appoint the oldest firstborn of all Claus siblings as reigning Santa.

Table of Contents

1 Lady in Waiting..1

2 Very Frustrated Lady in Waiting........................9

3 Lady Coveralls...17

4 Giving Birth Is A Handful!.......................33

5 Piece of Cake She Says!...........................47

6 Been Backstabbed by a Friend?.......................65

7 Hot Chocolate With Marshmallows!...............89

8 When Family Members War!...........................113

9 The First Shoe Drops...........................127

10 Righteous Women Bring Peace...................155

11 The Second Shoe Drops!...................159

12 Off Comes One Lace...........................173

13 Off Comes the Other!.........................185

14 Uh Oh Failure Now What?...............203

15 Picking Up Pieces Moving On.......................213

1
LADY IN WAITING

Who: Franken Jack Claus
Birthplace: Clausdom, North Pole
Occupation: Veterinarian; Primary Care
Provider
Degrees: Animal Husbandry; Medical
Father: John William Henry Claus
Mother: Mary Elizabeth Tor-Claus
Siblings: Bourbon Tor, Nicholas Henry
Wives:
--Elizabeth Anne (died in childbirth),
--Marilyn Lynn (died in childbirth)
Children: Frankie Anne Claus
Nephew: Junior Henry Claus

IT WAS THE MIDDLE of November in Clausdom; Thanksgiving was right around the corner for most North Pole inhabitants.

While Clausdom was the birthplace and home of the December holiday's acclaimed Santa Claus, this Thanksgiving time period was also widely celebrated in Clausdom.

The town-wide giving of thanks was considered an era of special blessing for them doing the Lord's work at Christmastime; when workers and managers alike, engaged in a week-long ritual of giving thanks for one another's Christmas work efforts for the year.

For most in Clausdom, blessing and being blessed was the rule of the entire November month; equally important as the giving of gifts on to boys and girls on Christmas Day.

Franken Jack Claus, kin to Santa Nicholas Claus, was the lone exception.

Yes, he was the older brother by several years of his younger Santa brother; his graying sideburns and balding head telling their own story. But this day for brother Franken was a day which would scar his heart forever. Blindsided, he was; and by the people he loved.

Besides the grayness enveloping his ears declaring the years betwixt the two, Franken Jack surpassed his younger brother in height as well; towering over the current Santa Claus by several inches.

Nevertheless, Franken's being older, his being taller and even his carrying thirty pounds less weight had nothing to do with his not being the reigning Santa. He was not Santa because he was different. The why of which, Franken had spent years putting behind him.

Right now, though, November events were taking a turn behind the scenes in the hallowed High Court of Clausdom; events and circumstances which would pit the ethics and morals of a Claus son against the Ten Commandments of Clausdom.

This particular Thanksgiving Day was not slated for Franken's cyclical giving of thanks. Indeed, it was to fastly become a unique, forlorn season; one which would define his destiny for the rest of his life.

TO SAY IT WAS downright frigid in North Pole's three remote regions would be a disservice to the word. It was ca-ca-ca-, c-o-l-d...cold.

If it wasn't freezing every day, it was still bitterly arctic with a sultry wintry frost overshadowing elves and animals alike.

In a word, everyone was miserable when caught outside in inclement weather. That is one reason all of Clausdom's citizens took great care to stay inside the Clausdom Dome when the bitterness of winter hit.

The other reason they stayed inside was for their own safety. Inside the Dome it was warm and safe.

Outside offered them naught but cold and isolated dangers in a harsh environment meant only for polar bears, walruses and seals.

The original purpose of the covering Dome was to hide Clausdom from the world-at-large; so the making of Christmas gifts could go on without interference.

With its off-white expanse in place, the Kingdom of Clausdom was securely hidden from the occasional observation plane scurrying overhead; one which used highly technical, aerial surveillance to detect and document unusual movement or activity on the surface of the North Pole.

The Dome's infrastructure was designed for survival purposes only, not for comfort;

though as was natural for those created by a God of coziness, certain polar amenities pleasing to one's flesh were not completely cast aside.

This year was turning out to be a particularly harsh start to a winter of freezing temperatures; anomalies when it came to the average coldness of November's early winters.

Such a degree of cold both inside and outside the Clausdom Dome made everyone miserable. Everyone, that is, except one Frankie Anne Claus; thirteen year old niece of the reigning Santa Claus. She loved it.

Frankie Anne was the one and only daughter of Franken Jack Claus; who, besides being the older brother of the currently reigning Santa Claus, was also the twin brother of the North Pole's most infamous citizen; one Bourbon Tor Claus.

Bourbon Tor was the Claus of infamy in Clausdom proper. This, because he is the only Claus in history to have turned his back on serving Christmas; doing so by rejecting the Ten Commandments of Clausdom.

Not only that, but along with showing Christmas his backside, his open contempt for the authority of the Twenty Four Elders of the High Court of Clausdom to rule over him was without measure.

This disdain of Bourbon's for Clausdom protocol was frowned on even more, because as the oldest of three brothers and the oldest twin, more had been expected of him in the way of service.

Thus it was firstborn Bourbon Henry Tor Claus moved out of Clausdom to the subterranean artic region now called TOR; rightly labeled after his mother's family. It was them mostly, who had worked the lower level mines in the secluded region.

In making his abrupt exodus from Christmas Clausdom, Bourbon slung dung in the face of the Elders by dropping his Santa father's middle name of Henry; thereby allowing his mother's surname to hold the true essence of his firstborn heritage.

In casting the name aside and moving to the Region of TOR, he cast aside all hope of ever being appointed the reigning Santa Claus of Clausdom by the Twenty-Four Elders.

The deed was done; the smoke had cleared. The eldest of three Claus sons was now known only as the infidel Bourbon Tor, a Claus in name only; Christmas outcast and persona non-grata in North Pole's Kingdom of Clausdom.

But for him, all was not over.

He was out, all right; but he was far from being down for the count.

A slow burning, deep down need for payback was brewing. His heart came to covet fulfillment of a rising vengeance; one which would settle the score with a certain number of Elders, and for anyone occupying the Santa seat which rightfully belonged to him as the eldest of three Claus sons.

Bourbon Tor's rising rebellion tailed by fierce-green jealousy would not only bring him to the brink of destruction in the end, but his un-Christmas-like efforts would ultimately bring Christmas Clausdom itself, to the brink of extinction.

A Frankenclaus Book!

2
VERY FRUSTRATED LADY IN WAITING

IN THE BARN, FRANKIE ANNE wasn't miserable from the frigid weather for one reason. She was in her father's birthing stall doing what she loved doing best.

She was taking care of a pregnant reindeer mother; doing the needful with her father, whose job it was to oversee the birth and provide workarounds for any complications.

Frankie's job was to provide lots of love and empathy for the mother; whilst her father took the reins of care when it came to the birth. This birth, however, was proving to be stormier than others she had seen.

Her father was both veterinarian and physician by Clausdom trade; a vet because of his love for animals; a physician because of the need for special needs practitioners.

Today, however, he was mainly veterinarian. And that was because the reindeer patient before him had four legs and not two.

Young Frankie wanted to be a vet just like her father, when she was of age to become one. Unlike her father, she only wanted to take care of sick and hurting animals; leaving the treating of people issues to others called to do so.

When her father was doctoring persons in Clausdom, Frankie Anne wasn't allowed to be present, for privacy reasons. This, of course, was fine by her. She was an animal person.

With animals, it was different. Where her father was going, she was soon to follow.

Her doctor father didn't mind her tagalong tenacity. It had been that way since his daughter could walk. She saw everything; no holds barred.

Truth be told, as a widower with one child, Father Franken wanted his daughter with him all the time. Daughter Frankie was the only one who truly understood his love for animals. Thus, she came to love animals as much as her father did; which is saying quite a lot when it came to the disfigured ones born different.

So it was Frankie Anne was the spitting image of her father; if not in physical looks, most certainly in spirit and soul.

When it came to appearance, though, she was short; he was tall. She was skinny; he was lean, with muscles bulging betwixt their sockets.

From a bird's eye view, Frankie Anne had a full head of almost all-black hair, while the central part of the brown hair atop her father's head was missing.

The sides were there, of course; but that was about it. To the eyes of an eagle on the hunt, he was bald to a tee.

About the face, her father was normal; save for the purplish spot on the right cheek; a carryover from a troubled birth. Some in Clausdom blamed the mark on his being in the womb with Bourbon; though Franken never thought that at all.

Anytime Frankie's father spoke of his daughter's features, his eyes never failed to twinkle; this was because she looked the spitting image of her mother; the love of his youth.

Her mother, he said, was similar in appearance. She had the same dark hair, the same depth of green around the eyes, and was surrounded by the fairest of tanned complexions; similar to the natural tan which Frankie sported.

Had her mother still been alive, Frankie's father said, the two of them would have been mirror images of one another in Clausdom society.

Sadly enough, Frankie Anne's mother crossed the high snows to Heaven the day after Frankie was born. This was due to unexpected complications arising from a childbirth filled with setbacks.

Unfortunately, her father later explained, the inevitable and unexpected occurs on occasion; taking everyone by surprise.

In her mother's case, the internal bleeding refused to be abated; calling for a Christmas Miracle; which didn't come. And no one knew why. It happens, they said. And for Frankie, that about summed it up.

Not even the magical anointing of her grandfather, the reigning Santa at the time, had been able to save Frankie's mother from giving up the ghost.

Mother Elizabeth Anne Claus passed from this life to the next, hours after giving birth. Before passing, however, she had the opportunity to hold her newborn close to her; showering the baby with love and tears she prayed would last a lifetime.

When alone and in bed at night, Frankie Anne's thoughts often drifted towards her father's words; of her being held by her mother; it being her mother's last request as long as possible; till the end.

The end for Elizabeth Anne was not longsuffering in coming. Cuddling her baby to her breast, Frankie's mother realized she was drifting off; her focus was awry and stayed that way. She could only feel her baby's face, not see it as before.

She prayed her final blessings of protection over her child. Afterwards, the room quiet, those who were there recalled a spiritually serene calm enveloping her mother's presence on the bed as a soft cloud.

Her mother's spirit rose out of her body without hesitation, leaving the shell of the body behind; lying on the bed. All knew her time had come; her time to ascend into the spiritual realm of the afterlife, where the Gates of Heaven awaited her.

BUT THAT WAS THEN.

This was now.

As the firstborn of a Claus son, the newborn infant had been named after both father and mother. She was Frankie Anne Claus; now and forever. The namesake had been decided upon by her mother, before her passing.

From a distance, some wondered why her mother hadn't elected to name her baby girl Jackie Anne Claus. The first letters of each name would have matched up then. But upon the mother's passing, no one opted for a change; hence, Frankie Anne Claus, it was.

If she had been a boy, she would have been named only after her father. Being a girl, though, sort of deluded her Claus namesake for being a candidate as Santa.

That was because as a female, she could never take on the office and duties of the Christmas Santa; or so it was said.

Growing up, Frankie dreamed otherwise.

This gender protocol, biased as it was against females, was customary in North Pole circles; it being in keeping with the unwritten traditions of the Twenty-Four Elders of the High Court of Clausdom.

Without a mother, teenager Frankie had grown up without brothers and sisters; the unique by-product of being raised by a single parent who loved her beyond words.

She was Franken Jack Claus' only daughter and only child; the heralded firstborn of Franken Jack's Claus family line. And as such, her father was proud of her well beyond measure.

A Frankenclaus Book!

3
LADY COVERALLS

ON THIS particular barn-lit night, Frankie was assisting her father-doctor with the birth of a baby reindeer calf.

Doctor Franken was an animal rights advocate; which is to admit, it was often declared he loved animals more than people.

And because he rarely dispelled the accusation, the animal lover was often characterized as Doctor Frankenclaus behind his back; that was when gossips hid behind gossamers to slur the truth of a matter.

The birthing of animals of any kind always fascinated Frankie Anne, having seen her first live birth in a barn when she was but four years old.

She didn't understand a lot of what she saw, but her curiosity in wanting to know more was sure peaked to the high hills.

Frankie Anne was a teenager now.

She had not only seen her fair share of animal births since the early age of four, but she had been regularly assisting her father with reindeer births in particular, since the day she turned seven; her age of accountability.

For a full five seconds now, there had been no sounds uttered in the freshly cleaned stall where new birth was about to burst forth.

The peaceful quiet was soon broken by the bellowing of Lady; the baby calf's momma.

Lady was primed in motherhood, about to give birth to the first calf of the month in Clausdom proper.

Being the first was considered a prosperous blessing during the month of one's giving thanks.

On his knees at Lady's hindermost feet knelt Frankie's father; dressed in the same red and white coveralls with complimentary black cuffs and hems Claus sons had worn for centuries, in the Christmas workshops.

Only the shirts they wore changed each day.

This particular day, Doctor Franken wore a purple shirt with the long sleeve buttoned tightly on his left arm, whilst his right arm was bare to the elbow.

Off in the corner of the straw-riddled stall, stood Frankie Anne; the top of her hair safely covered with an olive green scarf which matched her eyes.

The scarf was intended to protect part of her head from the splattering side effects of a reindeer mother giving birth.

Her attire of coveralls and purple blouse matched her father's work attire, by design.

The fact it matched his and carried the standard colors of the Christmas Santa's apparel was noteworthy to young Frankie Anne.

Though to be honest, her feminine attire was more of a customized raincoat design than true coveralls; to Frankie's way of thinking at least.

The coveralls had ties down the sides, holding down water resistant denim which enveloped her entire body. Betwixt every other tie was a flap of padded denim doubled up; for warmth and for protection; in case one of Lady's legs went where it shouldn't.

Frankie herself would have patterned her attire differently for such occasions as live births, but she didn't complain; knowing it was actually her mother who had first created the colorful outfit for her father.

At the same time, Frankie was told, her mother designed a matching outfit for herself; one which was notably more feminine. From a distance in Clausdom, it was said, all could see she was the wife of a Claus son.

Frankie's outfit was thus patterned after her mother's. And just as her mother helped her husband with live births of every kind, so too did Frankie now when and where she could.

Personally, young Frankie didn't think she needed such elaborate coveralls, but her father insisted on its use as a ticket to get into the stall. So, as an obedient assistant, she did as she was told.

AT THE PRESENT TIME, Frankie's arms were seen to be firmly wrapped around her quivering shoulders.

The upward movements of her chest showed the worry rising from within, most notably at the sight of the mother's ongoing inner trauma in giving birth.

This birth, unlike so many others, was proving quite tricky; giving her veterinary father fits at what he had to deal with. The turmoil stemming from the reindeer mother's insides was intense and at times, non-stop.

Doctor Franken took in the sight of his shivering daughter.

He shook his head at the general under-sightedness of maturing teenagers; those whose plight it was to struggle to hold onto sanity, whilst fighting off the turbulent emotions of a changing environment housing that sanity.

"I told you to bring a thicker under-shirt, young lady. You should have listened to me. We've been here before. The more difficult ones take time. You know that."

"Too late now, Father," she said; shrugging her shoulders to cast aside his concern. "I'm not leaving and missing Rose Petal's coming out party; no way."

Rose Petal was what Frankie had already named the calf early on; being sure the calf was female.

She used the name often when she had prayed for Lady to have an easy time of it; which she was most definitely not having.

"You won't miss the birth, Missy. Now, do what I tell you to do. Run get yourself a sweater or something warm; you've got time. The mother is ready but she's not ready. It's funny how every reindeer pregnancy is different. Some births are an avalanche; others are like a stick stuck in mud."

"It must be mud today, Father. I don't see why it takes so long to give birth anyway."

"Neither do I, child; but it does. God works in mysterious ways sometimes."

Frankie took a step towards the stall's now open gate.

"You would think when a mother's time had come, all a person had to do was to get her into position, grab hold of the calf and pull her out, and be done with it."

"What about the afterbirth, my young vet?"

"You mean the stuff that comes out after? Why, we'd just let the mother mess with the rest; like they do in the wilds outside the Dome. Then we could walk out five minutes after the birth and get warmed up by drinking a ton of hot chocolate."

Doctor Franken's cheek's split wide in a spirit of good humor; like his daughter had just told a joke. "Five minutes, huh?"

"That's what the old timers say in them stories they like to tell. They say things were different back in the old days; births were easy and living was hard. Now it's living which is easy and birthing which is hard. They weren't fibbing, were they?"

"I guess not. But you have to understand, young lady, conditions were different way back then. There were plenty of veterinarians around to hand-feed the mothers during each month of their pregnancy. That's not so much the case now."

Frankie's eyes widened with curiosity.

"Why not?"

"Well, for openers, we've a shortage of good vets willing to take the time to attend to the needs of a difficult birth. After all, to most folks it's just a reindeer; and we've plenty of those running around here in Clausdom. Some even say we've too many of these critters; they want to start thinning the herds."

"I've heard the talk. That's not good," Frankie's ponytail swished from left to right.

"It's not. But as it stands right now, there's Elder talk in Clausdom of forcing all of us to backtrack somewhat to the old methods of keeping populations balanced. It's a sore subject with those of us who really care about the animals with special needs."

Frankie said, "They'd be the first to go when push came to shove. I'm sorry, Father. Perhaps I misspoke earlier."

"I do agree with you on one thing, young lady. My job as a midwife would be a lot easier on me if every reindeer baby did come out in five minutes."

"It would be easier on the mother, I think."

"True enough, but a small percentage will always have a more difficult time of it. Unfortunately here in Clausdom, the ratio seems to have been reversed; we've more problematic births than smooth-flowing ones. It's been brought up before the High Court of Clausdom more than once."

Frankie's looked at her father, "Oh? I hadn't heard. I wonder why?"

"I suspect too much experimental breeding has a lot to do with it. A major side effect is a string of live births which are notably harsher on mothers in weak condition. I told your Uncle Nicholas as much."

"You did?"

"I gave him my two cents worth anyway."

"What'd he say?"

"The usual; he stonewalled me. He hinted how the High Court's Twenty-Four Elders had other ideas on it, but he was a closed mouth when I asked him for details."

DOCTOR FRANKEN DIPPED his hands in the bucket of warm water he'd brought in for Lady.

Grabbing a towel, he said, "I just hope this baby calf makes it out by morning."

Lady took that moment to rear up her head in a shout, signaling her own displeasure in how the long the birthing process was taking.

Doctor Franken shook some of the grime off the smock he was wearing. "Stroke her neck, Frankie. Talk to her. Try to calm her down."

Frankie Anne leaned close to Lady's ear.

"Easy girl," she whispered softly in Lady's ear whilst running the palm of her hand along the reindeer's mane in stroke after stroke.

"Father? Do you think it's because Lady's mother is a dino, she's having such a difficult time? That's what the elves in the workshops believe. Sometimes I overhear them telling each other how a dino is by definition, worthless, deformed and a no-account."

"I've never liked the term dino. It started as a nickname and turned into something sour. But, to answer your question, Missy, a mother dino's deformed physical makeup will on occasion affect a live birth; but not this time; not with this mother. She's only flawed with her coat discoloration; nothing else."

Frankie stood. She walked over to a post atop of which was a basket of once-warm cookies, now grown cold and hard to the touch.

Reaching in, she shoved half of one into her mouth and chomped down hard; thinking all the while of her father's words.

The cookie mostly gone, she muttered, "You mean Lady's considered a dino because she's spotted and not uniform in color."

"Exactly; which means her flaws are only on the outside, not on the inside; like me and my big-time birthmark folks look away from when they talk to me."

"They do that? Look away?"

"They do."

"That's sad. It must hurt when it happens."

"Not anymore, it doesn't. It's not my problem anyway; it's theirs."

Frankie decided it best to change the subject.

She already knew how Clausdom folks felt about one of the Claus sons having a notably large birthmark on the right side of his face.

It had cost her father his being appointed Santa.

She said, "Father, Lady's calf will be okay when it comes out, won't it? That's what you're saying, right? Dino mothers don't have to have dino babies. Rose Petal will be okay; right?"

Frankie Anne shoved a second cookie, a small one, into her mouth and reached for a third.

Her father said, "If I have anything to say about it, she will be."

Lady jerked her head around erratically for the umpteenth time.

She wasn't happy.

Frankie asked, "Why's she doing all that bellowing, Father? Doesn't she know all she has to do is grunt and push? It's supposed to be tons easier on reindeer mothers. I've never heard one cry out as much as this one."

"I thought you were going to help, Frankie."

"I am helping, aren't I? What's more, I'm freezing the tips off my toes. I'm going to double up on socks next time we do this. Is there something in particular you want me to do? You and Lady are doing all the work."

"Well, hello? I can't be in two places now, can I?"

"What's that mean?"

"It means you got to stop eating cookies and get back down on your knees. I can't be at her head comforting her, and down here at her feet delivering her baby. Sit yourself back down just above her head where you belong. You know the drill."

Frankie Anne did as she was told. Once positioned, she said, "Okay, I'm here."

Her father nodded with his chin towards Lady's head.

"Now, stroke her forehead again. Speak softly to her and don't stop. But don't lean over her like you're doing. She might rear up at a painful contraction and I don't want you getting hit in the head. Then I'd end up with two patients and we'd both be birthed with headaches."

His daughter tilted her head, cheeks widening at the danger she'd put herself in; she knew better.

She was just getting tired of having been doing the same thing over and over for such a long time.

It must be terrible for Lady, she was thinking.

"I'll be careful, Father; don't you worry none about that. Personally, I think Lady wants this over as much as we do. She should already know once she pushes the baby out, we'll leave her alone so she can love on her baby. It's not like this is her first baby and all."

"She knows the routine; don't you fret about that," Doctor Franken said. "What concerns me is how there is way too much whining going on with the momma."

"Too much? Pregnant mothers whine all the time."

"If you listen closely, Frankie, you see the sounds of trauma she's making are different than the ones we normally hear. Something's wrong with her and I don't know what it is."

"I suppose this is another one of those go-by-the-book deliveries, huh, Father?"

"As much by-the-book as we can, anyway. We'll go as slow as the mother wants to go. Though, maybe towards the last we'll pitch in and help a mite."

Frankie rocked her buttocks back and forth like she was on a horse. This sitting on her haunches was hard work when it took so long.

She said, "I'll vote for anything to ease her pain and mine. She appears to be almighty uncomfortable. You'll never find me taking this long when I have my baby, Father."

Her father's eyes shone with pride, "Oh? Tell me more, oh wise Santa sage."

"When I get pregnant and my time comes, I'll push my baby out, lickety-split in less than an hour; and you can take that to the Arctic Bank."

As if to put emphasis to her statement, Frankie reached over and rubbed Lady's belly; as if in doing so, the baby would just fall right on out. It didn't.

Having failed to encourage the delivery process and prove herself an expert to her father, Frankie Anne relaxed her entire torso backwards this time; turning somewhat at an angle in an effort to freshen up both hips at the time.

A Frankenclaus Book!

4
GIVING BIRTH IS A HANDFUL!

DOCTOR FRANKEN'S facial features broke into a widening smile; one which warmed as his cheeks peaked his temples.

What his daughter didn't know, she'd one day learn. Making babies was a lot easier than giving birth to one. And he couldn't help but tell her so.

"Frankie, my dear, you're growing fast but you're only thirteen years old now."

She interrupted, "Going on fourteen, Father; I'm getting closer every day."

"Almost fourteen, then; the point is, Missy, one day it will be you pregnant with child, with Lady watching on. It will be me and her listening to you hollering and carrying on so. You might even do some whining of your own."

"Not in a thousand years; not like she's doing now."

"When the time comes, young lady, I do believe you will find you and Lady have more in common than you think."

"Surprise, surprise, surprise, Father; I don't intend to get pregnant. Ain't no boy ever going to touch me. And if they do, I'll get out the shears and cut their cord."

Her father grimaced. "Frankie, what say we leave the shears out of it; shall we?"

"If you insist; I don't expect to need them anyway. Have you forgotten? As the oldest Claus sibling, I'm next up to be Santa when Uncle Nick retires. "

"I have not forgotten. I was up to be Santa once, myself. But it didn't happen. I was passed over."

"It will happen for me. The Twenty-Four Elders have no one else to choose."

"I'd not tell them that just yet; not if you don't want a comeuppance. They are old school; way old school."

Frankie said defiantly; her brow forming wrinkles, "I will be Santa Claus. It's my destiny. And when I'm Santa, I'm going to be much too busy to get pregnant. To my way of thinking, my giving of gifts to boys and girls on Christmas Eve is more important than me getting courted and getting pregnant."

"Spoken like a true, North Pole Claus, my dear. Your Uncle Nicholas would be proud of you. Just don't forget in all that enthusiasm of yours, there has to be someone who takes over as Santa after you; when you are the one who is old and gray and being forced into retirement."

"I guess I'd let Junior take over as the Claus Santa when I retire. He's younger than me by three years. I reckon he could do the job by the time I get my first gray hair of a winter."

"Don't get ahead of yourself, Frankie; things sometimes change. What happens if something unforeseen occurs and Junior crosses the high snows whilst you're still Santa?"

"Huh?"

"He'll be in Heaven and they'll be no Claus offspring left to carry on the Santa mantle. Christmas will be ruined forever; all on account of you not wanting to be in the same situation as Lady here. Christmas would be ruined. Boys and girls the world over would be in tears come Christmas morning."

"I never thought of that, Father. It is just me and Junior left, isn't it? Maybe you're right about me having at least one baby. I'll have to think on it some."

"You'd best think on it a lot. And if you forget, the Twenty-Four Elders will be quick to remind you of your motherly duty to the Claus lineage. By the way, when we're done here, don't let me forget I promised your Uncle Nick I'd stop by his house before bedtime."

"It will be late. You sure he will be up?"

Her father shrugged. "He says he's got something important we need to go over. I told him I'd be there regardless of the hour. He said if he was in bed, he'd get up; no problem."

Frankie clapped generously with undue exuberance. "Maybe he's going to ask your permission to let me ride with him on the Christmas sleigh this year. He can teach me the ropes of delivering gifts on Christmas Eve."

ONCE AGAIN Father Franken's eyes twinkled. His daughter had a one-track mind when it came to her becoming the official Santa of Clausdom.

It was a long shot, he knew, but he sure wasn't going to be the one who discouraged her. On the other hand, he had to set her expectations so she'd not fall off the deep end if things didn't go her way.

His daughter being a girl aside, she deserved her chance at Santa-hood. This was, after all, the 12st Century.

Women could vote.

Women could own land.

Women could drive a car.

He saw no reason why one couldn't be Santa for one night of the year. That being said, he still had his fatherly duty of protecting his daughter from the obvious.

"Frankie Anne, I need to remind you of something while we're on the subject of you being a Santa Claus."

Frankie looked up, wide-eyed; allowing her father to see the true depth of her emerald green eyes.

"Yes?"

"Permit me to remind you of what's on the table. Nicholas is Santa. And he has a son."

"He's younger than me."

"I know he's younger than you, but not by much. You can go as far up that Santa dream pole of yours all you want, and I'll support you to the hilt; but hold onto reason whilst you're there."

"Reason, it is, Father."

"Good. The point is, your Uncle Nick's ten year-old son will be seriously considered as a Christmas candidate by both his father and the Elders. And yes, it is because he is a boy and not a girl."

"Yeah, I know. I might be completely stubborn at times, Father, but I'm not totally blind. I know he's got the upper hand."

"The thing is, by the time he's old enough, Junior might want to become the next Santa before you. After all, his father is the reigning Santa and Junior is his firstborn son. And you know Clausdom tradition. Santa Claus responsibilities are generally given only to boys."

"I consider young Junior all the time, Father. He's just a baby. He can't do what I can do. I'm stronger and smarter."

"I can't argue with you there."

"And I do more work," she added. "I can also carry a full stack of wood into the house as well as milk the cows all on my own. As skinny and bony as Junior is, he can't do any of that. He gives up halfway through. I've seen him. He's too spoiled being Santa's son. It's made him soft, and not just in the belly."

"Yes, but some of that will change as he gets older. He'll put some meat on those bones of his. Him being a boy, he'll be huskier than you, too. And more than likely, with you being on the short side when it comes to height, Junior will end up being taller than you when the snow clears the rim."

"Not by much, he won't. I'm exercising every day and I'm working real hard to make my body as strong as any boy anywhere near my age. I'm not stupid, Father. I know being Santa isn't easy."

"I didn't say you were stupid, Frankie."

"No matter, Father; I know what you meant. But when my time comes, I fully intend to be ready to step into the Santa Sleigh and fly as high as the sky on Christmas Eve. By Clausdom Law, it's my right as the oldest living, Claus sibling."

Frankenclaus succinctly responded.

"Like I said before; you have my total and complete support. But it always pays to be ready for anything at any time; just let me say that as a side note of warning. You becoming Santa Claus is nothing I have control over; that ball is in the Elders' court."

Mother Lady's abdomen shook with a twist as Frankie held on tight.

"Whoa there, Lady," Frankie said. "Settle down. It won't be long now, girl. At least I hope not. Will it, Father?"

"You got my vote, Missy. I just need to point the limbs in the right direction. Right now, I can't even find all of them."

Doctor Franken's lungs let out a loud puff of warm air, his shoulders falling dismally as he pulled his arm from Lady's backside.

"Well, this is embarrassing. I don't know, Frankie. I can't quite figure out what's going on in there. I'm missing some pieces."

"You mean they are not where they are supposed to be, right? Is that why the mama's in a tizzy; because her baby's limbs are all scrunched up and causing her so much pain?"

"It has to be; I just wish I knew why it's as bad as it is. I'm missing out on something here. It may be a twisted leg, a deformed one or a broken one; I honestly don't know."

"Too bad we can't talk to her; like Uncle Nick does with his reindeer. I still don't understand why it's only Santa who can understand reindeer talk."

Her father chuckled. "It's all part of the anointing of being Santa. If you actually do get to be the first female Santa, you'll be able to talk to them as well. Right now, though, if I was Santa, I'd sure be talking up a storm with Lady about her baby."

"I'll bet. I think you should be Santa. You're older than Uncle Nicholas. It's your right. I've studied up on it."

"Let's not open that can of worms, young lady. Your Uncle Nick is Santa; duly appointed by the Twenty-Four Elders of Clausdom. I'm just a tired old vet trying to bring this baby out to stand on all fours. If your uncle was here, though, I'd have him ask the mama what the hang-up is."

"I still think you should have been Santa. Then I would most definitely be next in line to be Santa, according to Clausdom tradition."

"I know, child. But life doesn't always turn out the way we want it to. Sometimes, we just have to..."

FRANKIE HELD UP a hand to interrupt, twirling her eyes amidst an air of royal majesty.

"Hold it, Father, I got this one. Sometimes we just have to roll with the snowballs, right?" Her father had spoken those same words dozens of times over the course of her thirteen years.

"Why don't you roll with the snowballs and go get me the rope," her father answered back.

"Huh?"

"The rope, Frankie; run get the birthing rope, please. We're going to pull this baby part way out and I can't do it without the lasso in place. You'll find one hanging on the wall outside the barn door."

"Okay; back in a jiffy. I'm going to grab a coat while I'm at it, if it's okay. You want me to bring the cutter out while I'm in the office? I don't see it out here."

"What cutter?"

"The cutter, the slicer, you know; what you use to remove the body parts if the baby dies inside the mother when she gets hip-locked."

"She's not hip-locked. But yes, please do bring it out; and thank you. Not bringing it out earlier was an oversight of mine. I doubt we'll need it, but it's too smart a tool not to have around in a pinch."

"Of all the tools you use, Father, I hate that one the most."

"Me, too, dear; but if you don't want to take a chance on losing the mama as well as the baby if things go awry, it's a good tool to have close by."

"I don't like it because every time I see it, I remember how other vets in Clausdom use it on babies who are still alive inside the mother. It's mean and cruel."

"They only use it when they suspect the baby is deformed in some way, Frankie. It's tradition. It's the way it's been done for centuries. You can't put all the blame on present-day veterinarians for their ignorance. They're just following what their forefathers did in their day."

"Want to know something, Father?"

"Fire away."

"Some of the kids that are allowed to work in the workshops are saying Clausdom doctors use it on pregnant elves as well; to get rid of badly formed babies wanting to come out and take up space."

"I would think, young lady, you and your friends could find better things to do than discuss Clausdom's idiosyncrasies. Don't you agree?"

Frankie heard his words but ignored them.

"So, they really do it, Father? They use a cutter to slice a living baby to pieces while it's still breathing?"

"The device is only used on animals these days, Frankie; its counterpart is not used on elves anymore unless it's to save the mother's life. Obstetricians try to permit malformed babies to exit the mother naturally, if possible; as a means of protecting the mother's health from undue stress."

"And then they end its life?"

"They used to. Not anymore. I made such a fuss over it with the Elders; they put a stop to it. Deformed babies now have a right to live out their lives as best they can. The Elders didn't like me interfering, but because I'm a Claus son and we're few in number, they reluctantly agreed."

"I just hope they don't start up on it again. I'd hate to think of any of my relatives deliberately taking a deformed baby's entire childhood away from it."

"I couldn't agree more. You should know, though, the North Pole is unique; it's not the same south of the tundra. Some folks down south don't care if the baby is malformed or not. Even if it's perfect, if it's a girl, every other one gets put down. Boys survive; females cross the high snows."

"Why is that? What'd we girls do wrong?"

"Nothing. It's just that according to many world standards, boys are made for war. And there are plenty of conflicts cropping up these days. No one needs another cook."

"I can fight in battles; just as good as any boy if given the chance."

"I know. But as a girl, your battles are supposed to be in the kitchen and the bedroom, not on the battlefield. It's the way things have always been. It's tradition."

"Our ancestors again?"

"That's right. What they did, we do. That's the way it is. What us parents do, our children do. What I do, you do. Sometimes it's right and sometimes it's wrong. Life goes on, regardless. Me now, I'm helping this mama give birth. One day it'll be you on this end and me and my gray hairs codling the head on your end."

"I'm glad you're my parent, Father. Because we can be different and do things right all the time."

"From your mouth, child, to God's ear. Now, go get that rope, please. It's almost time."

"Lickety-split, Father."

A Frankenclaus Book!

5
PIECE OF CAKE SHE SAYS!

FRANKEN JACK CLAUS paused a moment, watching the hay strands fly from the clicking heels of his only child scurrying out the door. His daughter meant everything to him.

He was a Claus, and as such in Clausdom at least, he had privileges others didn't have.

Even so, he'd given up the luxury of living high on the hog at the North Pole; electing instead to spent his time and money on his beloved dino family of misshapen creatures.

That being said, there was nothing he knew which could take the place of his beloved daughter. Since his wife was no longer with him, he had only his daughter and his animals.

And while his animals were for the most part deformed in one way or another, Frankie Anne's natural beauty was the envy of the Dome; though she rarely dressed the part; preferring instead to tomboy-it-up for her dream filled role of Santa-hood.

Truth be told, she was his pride and joy. Though the Santa-hood part he privately put aside, knowing it was an uphill battle at best.

If they didn't want him to be Santa because of his blemished face, they surely wouldn't want his daughter because she was female. It had never been done.

When young Frankie returned, she tossed the entire rope towards his outstretched arm.

"One rope, as requested, Father. Catch. Want me at the head again?"

"Take the other end of this rope," he tossed one end back to her. "I need her tail tied out of the way."

"Piece of cake, Pop. Pip pip dee doo dah; pip pip dee day, I'm just the greatest knot tier in every way," she sang wistfully until done. "There; how's that, Father?"

"First-rate, young lady. I've never seen a better job of tying a knot. You'd best cinch it a tad bit higher up, though; just in case."

"If you insist," she said, grabbing the lasso anew. "I thought when you first asked for the rope, Father, you were going to wrap it around the legs and pull the baby out; expecting the head to follow. I forgot about the tail."

"So did I, honey. I should have tied it off first, when I could see she was having problems; but I was in a hurry to see what was going on inside the mother."

Frankie acknowledged his admission. That was one thing she liked about her father; he always told her the truth; even if she was just a teenager.

"You broke your own rule, Father. That doesn't happen often."

"Broke my own rule, I did, young lady; and let that be a lesson to you. You learn from my mistakes. A vet has to have patience at all times when it comes to cows giving birth. You should memorize that, Frankie, for when you're the vet and working on this end of things."

"I'm going to be a vet, all right; but I don't think I'll have much time for delivering calves. I'll be too busy being Santa. I've never seen Uncle Nick deliver a calf or a fawn."

"He's delivered plenty in his day. He wasn't always Santa. In his early days, we had fewer veterinarians here in Clausdom; so he delivered quite a few."

"And that was before he was Santa?"

"It was. He didn't have the gifts which came along with his being anointed Santa back then. Nowadays, of course, he can talk to animals. So if I'm backed into a corner on a delivery, I'll ask him to stop by and ask the cow to define the problem."

"I've seen him stop by; I just didn't know it was to talk to the cow."

"I don't know everything, honey. Your Uncle Nick is my go-to person when the oddest of problems arise. He's got the gift; but he hardly ever uses it with my animals, because he's too busy being Santa."

Frankie shrugged her head until her shoulders touched her ears. "Yeah, I guess that makes sense. He is Santa and can talk to them; so it's only fair to expect he'd be called in when needed. Why call on someone who can't talk to the mother, when you can call on someone who can?"

"I wish he were here right now with this one. It's taking too long. I fear for the cow's health. If we don't get this baby out soon, I'm afraid the mother will go into trauma or the calf will come out stillborn. Either way, it is not good for us or these two."

"I do have smaller arms, Father; if you want me to grab a leg. I don't mind getting dirty."

"Not this time, honey, but you are right. It's time you did learn; you're old enough. I would rather have you wait for a normal birth, though, for your first one." He looked at his daughter's face and understood her disappointment. He'd been there himself long ago.

He tried to soften the blow. "Don't worry; you'll get your share of tough ones. Right now, though, I'm going to get on my belly and inch my way into her as far as I can go. I'd like to see if I can feel the problem out 360."

"Let me know if I can help. I am thirteen now, you know. And Aunt Sarah told me you and Uncle Bourbon started doing deliveries when you were ten."

"Your Uncle Nick must have told her that."

"You started at ten and I'm going on fourteen and still waiting. Is it because you twins were boys and I'm a girl?"

"If you must know, it's because your first love is working in the Santa workshops with the elves. This is your second love, and that's where we differ, young lady. Working with deformed animals is my first love. Not that I wouldn't love the Elders making me the Santa; I would. But I'm happy where I am."

"I'm happy you are where you are, too. I do like our animals. They're different, but they're normal to me."

"Need a little help here, Frankie; hold her head taut while I slide my hand in, but be smart about it. One patient is all I can handle right now. Once I figure out what position the calf is in, we'll figure out what to do about it. There's a twist to the calf I don't recognize."

"Is it going to take long? That hot chocolate in the house is calling my name."

Doctor Franken grunted. "Yeah, well, being patient comes with the territory. You can learn that the easy way or the hard way; but learn it you will."

"I choose the easy way."

"Smart girl," he said; rolling to his opposite side. "My plan is to straighten out the front legs just a hair to set the neck in place. Then we'll position the rear legs so they're pointed towards the outside world."

"Is that it, then?"

"Often, that's all we need to do. We back off and hope the mother will do the rest. The less we do for her to get the job done, the better. She doesn't like us rummaging around inside of her."

This time Frankie grunted. "I'll bet!"

"Of course, if she's been going at it for too many hours and she's overly tired, we're forced to take action. That's when it could get rough on all of us."

"She looks tired to me right now," Frankie said. "Or maybe it's just me. It's already been an hour."

"She's not reached her breaking point yet. And it's only been forty-five minutes. You can just bet she wants this baby out of her as badly as we do."

"Now, that, Mister Vet, I do believe. I know I would want it out if I were her."

"If I have to, I'll speed the process by doing a little pulling while she's pushing. It might help matters."

"Really?"

"The important thing to remember, Missy, is you always want the mother to be fresh enough to do the bulk of the work. The only thing we do from the rear is to correct any positioning concerns and monitor what's happening. It's better for her. It's better for us."

"Maybe, Father, you should think about taking two baths when this is all over. You're getting to be an awful, smelly mess," Frankie crinkled her nose skyward.

A loud, guttural snort was heard. "Young lady, in another three years you'll be the one at this end. That's when I'll let you take the reins a hundred percent on these births. We'll see how sweet you smell when it's me comforting dear ole Mama's brow."

"I'll be sixteen by then. It'll be easy. I could probably do it now if you'd let me. But with the mess you're making going in, I think I can wait the extra three years."

"Don't talk for a minute, please. I need to focus on what I'm doing without distractions. The answer to all our problems is in her somewhere. If I can find it, we'll both be drinking hot chocolate in the house in an hour. This is getting to be work and it's getting to be mighty old, almighty fast."

"Whatever you say, Father. Let me know when I can talk. I got a pile of things to say."

"Hush."

FRANKIE ANNE found it amusing she was to remain quiet, whilst her father was allowed to talk up a storm.

He went on nonstop; itemizing every little move he was making inside the mother; almost as if little curios in his mind were on the tips of his fingers.

It suddenly dawned on her what her father was doing. With some of his words in-between the frustrations, he was actually teaching her particulars about the intricacies of birthing reindeer babies.

At the moment, her father was mumbling on; talking to the bones. "Now, where are you, legs? There's one. And there's another. Front or back, though, I don't know. Aye, there's the rub. Goodness! Well, that doesn't make sense."

"Something wrong, Father?"

"I found the legs but can't find a second joint on any of them. Something's wrong somewhere. Okay, Lady dear, let's do this by the numbers."

Frankie asked, "Want me to count?"

"I want you to be quiet. Where'd your head go, baby calf? Let's get it forward again. It'll be a miracle if this calf lives."

"Don't say that, Father. She will live. She has to. I've already named her."

Doctor Franken ignored his daughter, speaking to the cow instead.

"Oh, how I wish you could talk, Mother Deer. Oops, found a nostril. Sorry about that, baby deer. Blast it, Frankie; got a bad crook in my neck; I've got to move. This is not going to work anyway, doggone it. Okay, Mama, I'm coming out. Rest easy. I've got to take five."

As soon as her father cleared his arm and came to his knees, Frankie asked, "Want a bucket? And can I talk now? You want me to just drop everything and go get us some hot chocolate?"

"You can talk, sweetie. I'll get the bucket; you stay where you're at, though. I need to stand and stretch out the kinks in these old muscles of mine anyway." He grimaced as muscles contracted back into place.

He asked her, "You sixteen yet?"

"The longer I wait here, the closer I get," she smiled. "Can't you just grab the legs and pull on them like you did with the last one we delivered?"

"Well, yes, I could; if I was certain I had the back legs and not the front ones. I always look for the second joint on the front ones so I can straighten them out as a precaution. They must be tucked up under the calf somewhere, near as I can figure."

"What about the back legs?"

"I worked the back legs into position like they're supposed to be. They keep moving on me, though. Right now, I just need a minute to massage my neck before I go at it again. Then if she's ready, we'll hopefully commence with the final fifteen minute sequence and get this over with."

"Sac to feet, feet to head, head to shoulders; I got that part memorized by heart."

"You should. We've done this enough times."

"Does the baby feel okay inside?"

"Yes and no. The head is forward and best I can tell, so are the front legs. With the rear legs facing me, we should be okay. I just have to wait for her to start pushing, then I'll

57

join in and pull firmly on the legs; firmly but gently, I might add. We don't want to scare the mother."

Frankie asked quizzically, "Fifteen minutes, Father? That's about the length of time it's going to take me to have your first grandchild, isn't it?"

Her father laughed boisterously. "Maybe on your fourth one, Missy; it won't be on the first, I guarantee it."

"Fourth? Don't think so, Father. We only need one Santa Claus. So, I only need one child to take over for me when I'm done. Boy or girl, they're it."

"Sometimes, Frankie, life has a bowl of surprises just waiting for us to unravel. You may find you like being a mommy with the first one; then go back to the trough for seconds. It's been known to happen."

"Not with me, it don't," she whispered with a huff; eyes drifting to the loft above.

LESS THAN AN HOUR LATER, a newborn calf was seen squeezing out just like God planned; meeting the outside world with an unstable plop.

Once the calf was all the way out, Doctor Franken said, "Help me untie all the ropes, Frankie, and step back."

Frankie did as instructed. This was the fun part for her. After licking her calf clean, the mother cow always got up and moved to the other side of the stall; away from her baby.

This act on the mother's part forced the baby calf to rise to all fours, and take a deep breath as muscles came into fullness; allowing the calf to stand. Once on all fours, the calf would then hobble over to her mama for nuzzling.

Unfortunately, for all concerned, this normal coming up to all fours was far from normal; as only two legs were seen. This posed a problem. All fours was not to be.

It took father and daughter but seconds to discover a baby dino had been added to the citizenry of Neitherland.

"Oh, no," cried out Frankie.

"Oh, my, my, my," Doctor Franken said dismally. "That's what I feared the most; I just didn't want to put it into words."

"Where are the rest of her legs, Father? And the hooves? Did you leave them inside the mother?"

Her father tilted his head in her direction. "I didn't leave them anywhere. And don't look at me like that," Doctor Franken said sternly.

"Sorry; I know it's not your fault."

"You saw it same as me. The calf was born that way. But you're right; it wouldn't hurt to check to make sure the mother is free of extra parts inside. But what say we give mother and calf a chance to bond for a few minutes. Why don't you run in and bring us both back a cup of hot chocolate?"

Frankie almost jumped over the stall's gate. "You don't have to tell me twice."

She was gone before the words were out.

When fifteen minutes had passed and his daughter had not returned, Doctor Franken did the needful. He tied up the mother and ran his hand inside the mother, in search for missing parts to her calf.

Lying flat on his side again, he stretched his arm forward, fingers pulsating into hidden areas heretofore unreachable.

"It's a sad state of affairs; that's what it is, old girl," he said. "I don't like this anymore than you do."

Hearing noise aloft, he looked up. His daughter had returned.

She didn't have to ask what her father was doing; she knew what she knew. She only wondered if Lady knew it as yet.

Frankie moved around and behind her father's outstretched legs, studying the newborn calf with care. "Everything else about the baby calf looks healthy, Father. Though even if she had her front legs, it's obvious she'd still be a dino with them spots of hers."

Moments later, Doctor Franken stood up from his prostrate posture and shoved his right arm into the side bucket of water.

Without asking, Frankie grabbed a clean towel off the gate and handed it to her father.

Doctor Franken reported, "The mother's clean of limbs inside. So, I guess what we get is what we get. All things considered, I do believe we can save this one. Although, it's rather obvious we've a set of metal legs to make; before her hind legs forget they're supposed to walk."

"She's pretty, Father. Isn't she pretty?"

"There's none like her, that's for sure. You still going to name her Rose Petal, with her missing her front legs and all?"

"I think I will call her Ruby Red Rosie, because of her red nose. And even though her coat is spotted, it blends in perfectly with the lines in her face."

"How about just Rosie Red; make it simple and short; so the name fits her features."

"Rosie Red is perfect. You think the red nose is because of the bull?"

"Rudolph?"

"He's the father," she said.

"More likely, it's because of Donner, Rudolph's father. All his calves tend towards this same shade of red when it comes to the nose. It's in the genes, I suppose."

Frankie said, "Well, I think it's pretty."

Her father responded, "And I thank God we're almost done."

His daughter shook her head, "I'm done; you're not."

"Huh? Why?"

She raised her brow in his direction. "You asked me to remind you of your appointment with Uncle Nicholas. Remember? If it's important, you'd best not miss it. In the workshops, the elves have a dreadful fear of keeping Santa Claus waiting."

"That is understandable; he's their boss. As far as this meeting goes, I don't know if it's important or not. Your Uncle Nick said it was important."

"Then it must be important."

He chuckled, "Yeah, well, your dear old uncle thinks everything he does as Santa is important. We'll soon see; that's for sure. I'll leave just as soon as I get cleaned up." He reached for his cup of steaming chocolate.

"Is it okay if I wipe down Rosie?"

"Fine by me," he said. "Once the afterbirth is out, I'm going to leave. You can pet her all you want. Do try to remember to give Lady some alone time with her calf, please."

"You can count on it. When you're done there, Father, you might want to consider taking two baths instead of one; the first with water and the second with molasses. We don't want Uncle Nick having a sinus attack when you enter the Red House."

Her father went into one of his funny phases; continually making contorted faces resembling what his Santa brother looked like with one of his sinus attacks. He continued to make faces until the act broke out in love for his daughter.

"Two plus years," he said. "You've got two more years and maybe just one, if you keep on talking. And then it'll be you looking like this and smelling like this."

Seeing her father's widening grin, young Frankie felt overjoyed inside. It would be one year, she knew; because she'd keep on pestering him with every birth she attended.

She loved making him happy. He was, after all, the only one who truly understood and supported her dream of becoming the first female Santa Claus of Clausdom.

A Frankenclaus Book!

6
BEEN BACKSTABBED BY A FRIEND?

FRANKEN JACK CLAUS approached the Red House an hour after his daughter's red-nosed reindeer had been born.

Slung over his shoulder was his doctor's kit; it contained his tools of the trade for treating emergency animal issues. Where he was, it was.

The Red House was the official house the reigning Santa of Clausdom always resided in during his tenure as Santa.

This tenure's turn belonged to his brother, Nick.

It had been his for more years than Franken could count.

He had no idea why he had been invited; other than to officially fellowship with his youngest brother, Santa Nicholas Claus, the reigning Santa of North Pole's Clausdom.

Franken's knock on the front door initiated a short chorus of Jingle Bells being heard from above.

It was the character of the Red House to uphold the Christmas spirit in all aspects of architecture and infrastructure.

Santa Nicholas Claus opened the door a minute later; before the music stopped.

"Brother Franken, glad you could stop by. Welcome to the Red House; our home sweet home. Come on in."

His brother, dressed not in a Santa suit but nevertheless in colorful Santa attire, took a step back to let Franken in.

"I'm here like you asked, Nick. What's on your mind?"

"Not here in the doorway, Brother Franken; have a heart. Surely you've got time for a sit-down talk. We hardly see each other anymore. Let's meander on down to my private study."

Not waiting for a response, Nicholas Claus turned on his heel and led the way to a side room; bigger than most people's houses.

He appeared to be deep in thought; speaking not one word as he went down the side hallway towards his office in the west wing.

Franken obediently followed, as was obviously intended. He could do little else.

Though he was Nicholas' older brother, proper protocol demanded he remember his brother was the official Santa and he, Franken, was expected to yield to his brother's authority as a guest in the official Red House.

Once they'd crossed the threshold through the double door entrance leading to Nick's private abode, Franken walked on through whilst his Santa brother closed the doors securely.

Nicholas sat down in his ornately decorated Santa chair; the one which had belong to their Santa father.

"You can leave your trusty old, duffle bag under Sinterclaus' portrait, Franken. He can watch over it while you're here. Take a seat."

Franken Claus took his usual sofa seat; the olive green one. He had never liked it, but he still sat in it when in the Red House.

He found it amusing how the ugly chair presented a stark contrast to the purplish splash of a birthmark on his right cheek; something his Santa brother and others found most embarrassing for a Claus son to have.

"This must be important," Franken said. "I don't see any Clausdo doughnut's piled high on a plate."

"It didn't cross my mind this time. Sorry. I'll have the wife send over some, if you like. She loves cooking."

"How is Sarah? Healthy and happy as always?"

"She is. Though, like me, she is slowing down some with the years piling on."

"Me, too. Well, brother Santa, I'm a little off base here. Usually during these brotherly talks, you at least take the time to offer me a jelly-filled, glazed Clausdo as a way of buttering me up. You're off your game. What you've got to say must be something I don't want to do."

"I see you haven't lost your wit, Brother Franken. As a matter of fact, what I have to say is more important than your stomach; though I do apologize for the missing Clausdos."

Then, as though a light switch had just changed the direction of his thoughts, Santa-Nicholas told him, "If you don't mind, I think I'll stand and get the kinks out. I've been sitting most of the morning already."

"That's fine by me, Brother Santa."

IF FRANKEN had been a suspicious man, he would have suspected his Santa brother chose to stand while he himself sat, as a ruse to tower over his veterinarian brother.

Height was often used as a strategy by those in authority; to dominate those they intended to manipulate into doing something they didn't want to do.

Doctor Franken recognized the positional move, but was too relaxed and tired after Rosie Red's birth, to suspect his Santa brother had a hidden motive in the making.

As it was, Franken Jack remained where he was; immobile and somewhat uncomfortable.

He was ready to leave and his brother hadn't even gotten to the point in his speech yet.

He never liked visiting his Santa brother's private office.

The scenario for the two brothers was always the same; he was expected to remain quiet and acquiesce to the Santa-hood of his brother, while his brother gave a Santa speech full of the anointing Franken didn't have.

Twisting his buttocks around so as to follow Nicholas' steps, Franken admired his father's old office.

The well-padded sofa seat he now sat in was positioned directly across from his father's more grandiose, apple-red, Santa seat; with its ornamentally honed, mahogany arms.

If he recalled correctly, his father had built it; donating it to the Red House when he retired. It was then the Twenty-Four Elders had appointed number three son, Nicholas, to replace their father as the ruling Santa.

"So, Nick," Franken Jack asked, "why the suspense? What's so important we have to meet behind closed doors late at night, and forego the courtesy of hot chocolate and one of Sinter's triple-holed doughnuts?"

"You're the reason we're here."

"Uh, huh. Well, can't say I like the sound of that. What did one of my dinos do now?

Step on some Elder's imported roses from down south?"

Nicholas shook his index finger with firmness. "That is not funny, Mister."

"It never is when it comes to Twenty-Four Elders making command decisions which affect me and my animals. But, whatever; say what you have to say."

"There's no whatever about this. We've serious business to discuss."

"Everything is serious business with you these days," Franken said. "Okay, I'll bite. So which disabled group of mine is causing you problems this time? No, let me guess. It's the handicapped orphans who can't fend for themselves and have no one to look after them but me. Right?"

"There's no call for that kind of attitude, Franken. I'm trying to talk straight to you, brother to brother, Claus to Claus."

"Whatever," Franken retorted with his favorite word when it came to his Santa brother. Already tired of his short stay, Franken Jack again shifted his weight; this time from his right hip to his left.

A twinge of pain in his hips hit him; he winced, wondering if it was arthritis setting in.

He put it on his mental list to investigate the matter when he had time.

Santa Nicholas moved close in; making it so he towered over his seated brother all the more.

Once there, he asked, "Are you listening to me, Mister?"

Franken quickly picked up on the tone of the meeting.

His brother had gone from using proper names such as Franken, to evoking non-personal references such as Mister. The scent in the air was changing, and not for the better.

"If it's not the children I'm here for," he said, "it's my animals. And if it has to do with one of the deer I set up with prosthetics, accidents will happen. They have to get used to the wearing the devices. Mishaps are to be expected and I would hope, forgiven. I've told you this before and more than once, I might add."

Santa Nicholas walked to the end of the green and blue stripped loveseat off to his right.

Walking around to its back, he bent forward, leaning his protruding stomach atop it for support.

He then crouched low in Franken's direction, for emphasis of his next words.

"I'm well aware of what you've said on previous occasions. And to a point, I understand it. Prosthetics on humans is something I can forgive; but prosthetics on animals," he raised himself skyward, "prosthetics on animals are an abomination. That is something I cannot understand."

Franken stood as if to go.

His Santa Claus brother had just crossed the red line of proper etiquette.

In rising, he spoke louder than normal, "My animals are off-limits, Nicholas Henry. I think we're done here."

"Not by a long shot. Sit back down!"

His brother had spoken with Santa authority, so Franken did as told.

Nicholas said, "I've an agenda here. Open your eyes; you'll see a stir has risen in Clausdom about those broken-down dinos of yours."

Franken answered, "And just how is this supposed to be new News to me? A day hasn't passed when someone wants to squeeze out what little life a disabled invalid has left; just to get rid of the ugliness of dealing with them."

"This time, I'm afraid; it's mushrooming towards volcanic levels."

"Really?" Franken's brow upraised with a stir; warning bells going off betwixt his ears. "Perhaps, Nicholas, you'd best tell me the particulars of this new stir. To which deformed dinos are you referring; my crippled children or my prosthetic attired animals?"

Nicholas Claus smothered a moan as he sat down on the loveseat's arm.

He paused several seconds before going on, choosing his words with great care and purposeful intent.

"I think you're missing the point, Brother Franken. You got to look at the bigger picture, and here, you've gone and buried your head in the ice. You can't see the stars for the snow in what I'm trying to say. Here in Clausdom, a dino is a dino; period. Clausdom protocol is to breed us out of both dino animals and dinoelves."

"The perfect society, I believe it's called."

"There's nothing wrong in wanting to birth only children who have all their limbs and no health defects. We do it for animals all the time. And there's nothing wrong in wanting to shorten the pain and suffering of children being emotionally harmed by their physical shortcomings."

"What you're dreaming of will never happen; no matter how hard you try."

Santa Nick shook his head. "That's not true."

"A dino is a handicapped creature of nature. It isn't their fault they are born with blemished features or come out physically challenged. It happens in newborns because the physical is nothing more than an extension of the spiritual. And sometimes the spiritual is broken. That's the way life is."

Nicholas took a few steps back. In doing so, he said, "Times are changing in Clausdom, Franken Jack. You'd best get on board or be left behind."

"You didn't answer my question, Nicholas Henry. Which group of mine is causing this stir in Clausdom? Is it my dino calves or my dino patients?"

"Take your pick. In your perfect world, what applies to one should apply to the other; right? At a root cause level, both are the problem."

"Clausdom will never be a perfect society, Nicholas, no matter how hard you try. Dinos are here today; dinos will be here tomorrow. A dino is a handicapped creature of nature. And nature always has its flaws. It's not the dino's fault that nature blindsided some with deformity."

"Let's switch horses here, Brother Franken; I fear my point is being sidetracked. The dinos are a side issue, anyway. The DMAIC Team has determined the root cause of our present dino problem lies with you, not them."

FRANKEN JACK JERKED his head around; shocked.

With his brother standing his him seated, he felt like he was in a witness chair in front of the High Court.

The air around him had abruptly become stale and stuffy. He had to move.

With the admission by his brother of outside influences coming into play, Doctor Franken rose to his feet to meet his towering adversary head on.

"They have problems with me, do they? What did I do?"

He knew he was in deep trouble if the DMAIC Team had been summoned. "And what, pray tell, is the sigma analysis team doing looking into my affairs? Don't they have better projects to wet-nurse their time on?"

"They were given a project directive by the Twenty-Four Elders to define the root cause of low numbers coming in on gift-production processes."

"That sounds standard enough. It also sounds official. How does such a project involve me, though? I don't even work in areas of gift-production anymore. You know that as well as I do."

"I didn't say you did," Santa Nicholas huffed. "It's just that the DMAIC analysis has narrowed the cause for low gift production to the locals believing you're neglecting the spirit of Christmas."

Franken began to pace; shaking his head to sort things out.

"Impossible," he said. "Me being the cause of low workshop output of Christmas gifts is absurd to the point of being farcical."

"Welcome to my world, Mister. Truth be told, folks believe you're passing over Christmas in favor of all these dino-deformed creatures they consider not worth saving. It's anathema to them."

Santa Nicholas watched his brother's movements closely.

He was leading up to something and it had to be brought into the conversation at just the right time.

"It never bothered them before," Franken said.

"Well, it bothers them now. Look, Franken Jack, the problem is not so much with the dinos, as it is with you."

"Me, again; huh? It's always me. Woe is me," he crowed.

"In the past, everyone has ignored what you do. But it's a new century. People are thinking differently than we did in our day. Nowadays, folks have little patience with those they feel are neglecting the spirit of Christmas. It's become akin to blasphemy here in Clausdom."

Franken Claus said, "Blasphemy? That's stretching things a bit, don't you think, little brother? Now, you know I'm not against Christmas. I love Christmas."

"I know that," his Santa brother nodded.

"I love Christmas, but I also love crippled ones who need my care."

"I know that as well."

"I don't understand where this attack is coming from. What changed this year to get folks so riled up? I'm doing the same work I've always done."

Nicholas Henry moved closer, strategically maneuvering his limbs to take up residence on the higher part of the sofa directly opposite his brother.

Now face-to-face, Nicholas Henry pointed towards the picture of the Twenty-Four Elders covering the entirety of the North wall.

"Folks have filed complaints with the High Court. That is what changed. I'm afraid those dinos of yours have become somewhat of a red flag for the Elders."

"I hadn't heard."

"That's because you're out of the loop most of the time. You either got your head buried up the backend of a reindeer, or you're too busy welding a metal leg on a stump to notice what's going right under your very nose."

"Prosthetic legs aren't welded on, Nick," Franken said dryly.

"No matter; you are being flat-out accused of Christmas infidelity; that's what's at stake here. Stressed-out elves are saying you do more for derelict dinos than for Christmas Eve's gift-run success."

"My devotion to those with special needs has nothing to do with Christmas Eve, Nicholas Henry. It has to do with me caring for those who are less fortunate than the rest of us. It's my way of giving back. I have nothing against Christmas; but Christmas doesn't need another Claus. They have you. The dinos have no one, if not me."

"When I said times have changed, Franken, I meant it. You don't see it because you're never around normal people. We're busy here in Clausdom. Work-related anxiety has doubled. And when folks are stressed, they start looking for slackers. This year, your name is at the top of the list as Chief Slacker."

Doctor Franken snorted his displeasure at being accused so.

"My name shouldn't be anywhere. Christmas doesn't need another Claus. They have you. The dinos have no one, if not me. I'm the only doctor who will work on them. The only thing the other vets around here want to do is to put them down."

"It is tradition."

"Look, Nicholas, please tell me exactly what is being done by me that bothers folks so much? And just give me the high points, please; I don't need a full blown Santa lecture. I get those enough."

"Human Resources say the workshop assembly line workers are being overworked to the breaking point because of the world's exploding population. And here you are, doing nothing with your Claus Anointing to help them out. They're offended you don't see they are hurting, and do more for them with your Anointing."

"It seems to me these folks you are talking about are being unfair. I am a Claus but I am not Santa. I have no ownership of Christmas; remember? The Twenty-Four Elders sidelined me when they elected you Santa over me. You're the Santa; I'm the water boy. And I have my own life to live."

"Nevertheless, it's appearances that count, Brother Franken. Your working with the dinos has become a major distraction. The disabled children, now, I can understand you working with them; they're human. It's those ugly animals you're saving that bothers not only me, but everyone else."

"For Christmas sake, Nicholas Henry; they're innocent animals; helpless to the hand nature has dealt them."

"The worker elves don't look at it that way. The general feeling is these animals without limbs need to be put down."

"Yeah, over my dead body, they will. We went through this when I first started saving them. Remember how that turned out, little brother? Well, I'm still saving them, aren't I?"

"Chill out, Mister. No one is touching your animals as yet. To be honest, I don't know if you're the root cause of the problem or the scapegoat for the problem."

FRANKEN MOVED around to the back of his chair; his hands went down hard, gripping its backing.

His knuckles turned sour white, while his forehead wrinkled with folds declaring mounting pressure alongside his temples.

People were always trying to force him to put down his special needs animals.

It was a sore spot with him.

He said, "And that's why you invited me here today, isn't it? You want to discuss which is more important to me; my faithfulness to the dinos of Clausdom or my allegiance to Christmas itself."

"Exactly," Santa Nicholas said, sliding his backside to the rear of the sofa whilst spreading both arms wide across the top. He leaned back. "I can see we're on the same page now. That's good. This is going to be easier than I thought."

"My obligation to the handicapped is unchanging, Nicholas Henry. I'm as committed to helping those with special needs today, as I was when we were kids. Children or animals, it matters not. Both you, those dimwits complaining and the Twenty-Four Elders will just have to deal with it."

"Oh?"

"At the risk of repeating myself, Santa Sir, I am a Claus son but I am not the reigning Santa. I have a right to do what I want, if I am not good enough to be Santa."

"That's not what I want to hear. Even a Claus son with bad looks has his limits. Look, Mister, the Twenty-Four Elders told me to talk to you and bring all things dino, back into balance here in Clausdom. Those are the High Court's orders. As Santa, I am duty bound to follow them."

Franken Jack's words became sharper, revealing his rising frustration at the corner he was in.

"Not my problem," he decreed; his fast pacing renewed. "If they would have made me Santa instead of you like they should have because I'm older, I would have already solved the problem. I'm not a person who ignores obstacles and pitfalls."

Santa Nicholas said, "Why can't you confine yourself to being a medical doctor and working with crippled children alone? It's best for everyone."

"Not if you're a reindeer with a missing leg, it's not. They're the reason I'm both a medical doctor and a veterinarian. I do it all, for all; as long as they're disabled. No one is left behind. You're wrong in all this, Mister Santa Claus. Leave it be and leave me be."

"I'm just the messenger, Franken Jack. Don't blame me. I'm just doing my job as the Clausdom Santa. The Elders told me to talk to you and bring things back into balance. Balance is all I am trying to achieve here."

"The Elders again, huh?"

The words reeked from Franken's lips with a razor-sharp smugness intertwined with disgust.

"They do get around, don't they? I could use a drink."

FRANKEN JACK, by design, turned his back on his Santa brother.

His eyes scanned the furniture along the wall for what used to be the opening to a pull-out fridge; one which contained easily accessible water bottles.

It wasn't to be found.

It must have been removed during the last remodeling job, he reckoned.

As Franken's eyes continued scanning the walls, Santa Nicholas came himself to his feet testily.

"That's right, Franken, hit the bottle like Brother Bourbon. That's what he always does when there are important matters to discuss. You and him are more than twins. You are two of a kind."

"You can leave my twin brother out of this conversation, Nicholas Henry. He has his problems. I have mine."

Nick Claus fumed, "He's as much you as you are him! Can't you see it? You're both different than the rest of us. Don't you find that odd and yet, you two being twins, not so odd?"

Ignoring his younger brother's outburst, Doctor Franken approached the west wall to peer at an open crack.

He knew his Santa brother was talking about the purple blemish on his face, and the character default in his anti-Christmas twin brother.

He couldn't do much about either. Some things in life were out of his control.

His mind was going a mile a minute; his lips were dry.

He needed a drink.

On his own volition, he decided break the spell of the conversation by summoning a maid for hot chocolate instead.

He reached for a nylon cord which hung down from the ceiling next to it.

Grabbing hold of the cord, he yanked it hard three times before turning it loose.

Only then did he turn around to confront his Santa sibling with choice words.

"I'm ordering hot chocolate, Nicholas, not whiskey. You can relax and give your gray matter a rest. I'm not going to let you push me off the deep end of what I believe, no matter what you say about my dinos."

SANTA NICHOLAS CLAUS did relax.

He stretched out his legs full length on the sofa, to settle his posterior into the sofa's thick cushion.

"Fine, so be it," he said. "Order your hot chocolate. Order me some, too. I'm not going to let you drink alone."

Franken looked towards the closed doors, wondering for a split second if they were locked. He supposed not. Those against him weren't that desperate, yet; at least he hoped they weren't.

He waved a hand nonchalantly, sitting down anew. "Finish what you have to say. All of a sudden, I have a driving itch to be elsewhere."

"You have an itch? How about me? I got my own itch I'd like to get rid of; twenty-four of them to be exact. It irks me how I have to clean up after you time and again. You're my older brother, for Christmas sake. You're supposed to be helping me more than I am helping you."

"Whoa, there, Santa son; I never told you to be your older brother's keeper; for me or Bourbon. You should have just let well enough alone."

"I can't. I answer to the Elders."

Franken smirked as he spelled out the elephant in the room. "That's because you're S-a-n-t-a, Santa. It should have been me. I'm older than you."

A Frankenclaus Book!

7
HOT CHOCOLATE WITH MARSHMALLOWS!

AT THAT MOMENT, Miss Delores Tulip, one of the Red House maids, knocked twice on the door.

She then entered the room in her red and white, maid's dress and curtsied.

Both Claus men stood up out of respect.

"You summoned me, Mister Nicholas, sir? Is there something you needed?"

Before his Santa brother could respond, Doctor Franken spoke up in quipped fashion.

"No, young lady, your Santa Claus who hates animals doesn't need anything. I pulled the blasted rope. I would like a pot of hot chocolate and a plate of fresh, creamy Clausdos brought in post haste. I haven't eaten and it looks like I am going to be here awhile."

"I'll check on the Clausdom doughnuts, sir. I'm not sure how fresh they'll be, though. We've only frozen leftovers from this morning."

"Bring them anyway. I'll douse them in hot chocolate to freshen them up."

"Yes sir. And you, Mister Nicholas sir, would you like something while I'm here?"

"Just two cups with the hot chocolate, Delores; nothing more, thank you. And please forgive my brother the abruptness of his talk."

"Yes, Santa; I will do that."

When Miss Tulip left the room and her footsteps were fading, Santa Nicholas said, "Try to be more respectful of the House staff, Franken. How you feel towards me is not their fault."

"My apologies."

"Noted. And for your information, I personally don't particularly care what you do with those oddball critters of yours. As far as I'm concerned, when you're on your own time; you do what you want."

"I couldn't agree more."

"But folks know you're a Claus; there's a ringer there. They figure if you're a Claus, you should work as hard on Christmas projects as they do; more than ever when it's crunch time in the fourth quarter with no time to spare."

"I do work as hard as they do; just not when it comes to making gifts."

"You don't work in the way folks expect from a Claus son who carries the Claus Anointing. They want you to help them make December's fourth quarter ending a solid success; maybe even take the burden off them a bit by using your inherited Claus powers to lighten their workshop quotas."

"Christmas is many things to many people, Nicholas Henry. The way I see it, my dinos have a right to enjoy a Nice Christmas, too. I do things for them normal folks don't like doing; like wiping up dinodirt and tending to the more involved personal needs of bedridden children."

"Blast it, Franken," Nicholas cried out. "You keep throwing the animal dinos in with the human dinos. The two are different. The Elders separate their importance; you should, too."

"There is no difference. Not to me; I see them as one. They're both in need of my professional assistance."

"They are most certainly not the same. Besides, doing charity work for either dino animal or dino elf does nothing towards making the Christmas gift-run a success. We are Claus sons. The success of the Christmas gift-run is our highest priority."

FATHER FRANKEN WRINKLED his nose up high, like he'd seen the Elders do. He then tried to mimic the talk of an Elder.

"I've always believed the success of Christmas and charity work go hand in hand, Mister Santa. The greatness of Clausdom should be known for both."

"Don't patronize me, Franken," Santa Nicholas said. "What you call success is a slap in the face to those doing all the real work in Clausdom. What I know for sure is workshop production is suffering and all DMAIC inquiries point to you. The Elders asked me to speak with you about resolving the matter quietly."

"And so it's the Elders, as I suspected, and not you who is coming down so hard on me."

"That's right. I wouldn't be bringing this up if I didn't have to. As Santa, I'm caught in the crosshairs betwixt you and the High Court. It's not fair; to me. It irks me when I'm yanked into your messes and have to do cleanup. It's been that way ever since we were kids."

"Then don't do it."

"Look, Mister, when folks know you're a Claus, it just naturally follows folks figure you should work as hard as they do to make Christmas Eve a success. I didn't want to bring this up, but some folks think you should work twice as hard as them to make up for your ill-gotten twin."

"That is preposterous. Bourbon is Bourbon and I am me. And I do work hard; just not so much when it comes to gifts."

"Doing charity work for dinos does nothing towards making the Christmas Eve gift-run a success. And that, my friend, comes from the Twenty-Four Elders."

"Tending to animals as a veterinarian is my first love. It always will be."

"That's the problem. Christmas should be your first love."

"Do the Elders know I've only extended my work to include the treatment of malformed elves because few of the doctors in Clausdom are inclined to help the physically or mentally challenged? It seems those with special needs soil the image of Clausdom."

"Well, it didn't have to be you to see to their needs. You could have paid someone else to take care of them. If you offer folks enough money, they'll do most anything short of blaspheming Christmas. It's a sad statement, but it's true."

"Nick, Nick, Nick; if money is more important to folks than a broken child's innocent face, their heart wouldn't be in it. A poorly done job would be the result."

"Not necessarily. There are some good folks out there."

"Nevertheless, if I ignore the dino dilemma, I believe even more crippled children would be lost in the cracks than I'm losing now. Unlike those shop folks who are duty bound by an oath, I feel morally obligated to help boys and girls who are considered castoffs by societal norms."

Santa Nicholas said, "Our standards have to be high if Christmas is to survive. That comes from the Lord Himself."

"You know, Nicholas, when I first dedicated myself to helping the dinos, the malformed animals were being indiscriminately slaughtered, and handicapped elves were being closed off from public view. It was wrong. I had to do something to stop the travesty."

Nicholas Claus shook his head. "Right now, Franken, I'm only interested in discussing the dino animals you care for. That comes first with the Elders."

"My animals are doing just fine. They're not hurting anyone, especially a certain Twenty-Four Elders."

"For two thousand years, Clausdom has prided itself in raising perfect animals without spot or blemish. For two thousand years, we've bred animals to the epitome of perfection. Then you come along with a birth marked face and lickety-split, you develop a liking for the imperfect ones."

"That is me, all right. My face and those animals go hand-in-hand."

"You've made the entire system the Elders had set up, all wacky.""

"The system will survive."

"Are you telling me, Franken, you don't try to breed to perfection with your animals, same as us? Because we all know that would be a lie."

"I'm telling you, Sir Santa, I don't do what the Elders want done. Taking the deformed calves out to the tundra to die the day they're born is not breeding to perfection. It's killing off the ones you don't want because they don't measure up to your standards."

"The Elders simply want to follow tradition."

"Claiming you're breeding to perfection is you trying to justify murdering innocent animals and placing the helpless in harm's way. It's barbaric, cruel and a poor testament to the Claus family."

"It all depends on your perspective, Franken Jack. It's what our Father did with us helping him, if you recall."

"I didn't like it then and I don't like it now. Every baby developing in the womb with a shadow is not a Down syndrome baby expected to be aborted. Doctors need to stop lying to expectant mothers just to get rid of a potentially flawed child."

"I told you to leave the children out of this. What is your problem?"

"My problem is with Clausdom's way of doing things. Old traditions need bled out and new traditions need to be stitched into place."

"Our Clausdom tradition has never failed us, Franken. Tradition says to let the flawed ones die off. We both grew up in the same house, didn't we? You know what's normal and what's not, same as me."

"I do."

"Then you know helping special needs animals live longer instead of die off sooner, means more of them are on the streets staring us normal folks in the face. What you're doing is keeping them alive when they should be dead."

Doctor Franken said, "I'm keeping them alive because they have a right to live; same as you and me."

"It's an abomination. I may feel sorry for them, I'll admit, but I get a sick feeling in the pit of my stomach every time I look at them."

DOCTOR FRANKEN GRIMACED at his Santa brother's words.

Yet, he knew, they summed up how most Clausdom residents felt about seeing his disabled animals in public; especially those with metal prosthetics attached to them in sundry places.

He said, "Just be Nice to them, Santa, and they'll be Nice to you. Try being a Nice Santa to my animals for a change." Franken eyes beamed; he knew he was right.

Not surprisingly, his Santa brother took the opposite stand.

"How can I? When every time I turn around, I'm tripping over a metal leg or rubbing against a plastic arm in a crosswalk. It's gross."

"Oh, it's not as bad as all that, Nicholas Henry."

Santa's voice got louder.

"It is too. You got so many patched-up dinos running around; normal folks like me have to step around their curved prosthetics just to walk down a straight sidewalk!"

"Nicholas Henry, I have never agreed with Clausdom protocol on disabled animals. I've not kept it a secret."

"I get the feeling I'm beating a dead deer here, Franken Jack. I've tried several directions of approach to make you understand what's on the table. You just don't get the importance of what we're talking about. Let me try something else, from a different direction."

"You got my vote," Franken said.

"You listening?"

"I've been listening."

"Good. Now, standard protocol for Clausdom is traditional in scope. You know that same as me."

"I do."

"Man's allowing only the fittest animal to survive has been going on since baby Jesus was born perfect in a manger. You shoot a horse with a broken leg and you put down a calf with a broken hip that can't walk. Agreed?"

Franken ignored the question.

"If our forefathers did wrong, should we do wrong? I think not. Indeed, we should correct the wrong. For me to allow animals to suffer through lack of proper care is an abomination before God. I didn't become a veterinarian just to watch them die."

"Franken, Franken, Franken," Nicholas Claus lamented. "Don't you understand? It's normal for us to ignore the more inferior creature in favor of those more perfect?"

"Not for me."

"Jesus told us to become more perfect like Him, did He not?"

"Like His Father, anyway."

"Whatever. The point is, sir, Jesus didn't tell us to multiply our imperfections like the devil. He said get rid of the imperfections; cut them off and cast them into the fire. Or better yet, press our hands down hard on their heads, and send them out into the wilderness with the sins of the people."

"I'm not sending any of my animals into the tundra."

Nicholas' hands flew skyward.

"Why are you being so stubborn? I'm getting a headache trying to explain this to you. Wake up, for Christmas sake."

"What's normal for others is not always right for us, little brother. We're Claus sons, remember?"

"Well, smarty pants, in case you forgot, killing off the unwanted is the purpose of selective breeding. And it's not like we out and out slit the throats of inferior animals like in the old days. We get rid of them the humane way; the tundra way. We let nature take its rightful course in their lives."

Franken said, "What you do is encourage them to have shorter lives, by standing by and doing nothing to prevent them from dying. And if they don't die soon enough, you take them to the tundra and leave them to the elements. To me, it's inhumane. Slitting their throats was probably more merciful."

Santa Nicholas let his weight fall on the couch hard.

Palms up, he said, "You think it's inhumane? Honestly, Franken, get real. You got to come into the 21st Century. We're in a new age of enlightenment; where the differences between light and darkness are more pronounced."

"How so?"

"How so? Well, duh, for openers, mankind is always breeding up. And I'm talking about animals here; not humans. What you're doing in breeding down; you're trying to save dinos is impractical in this new environment."

"What I'm doing is the right thing to do."

"How many times do I have to say it? You can't save these animals, Franken. After you're dead and buried, their plight in life will revert back to the way it was. They're still going to live short lives. They're still going to die. Nobody cares about them. Don't you see?"

"I don't deny what you're saying, Nicholas Henry. But someone has to make a stand on their behalf. It might as well be me."

"There's nothing in life for them, but to live humpty-dumpty lives. And they're still going to live shorter lives. And why? Because it's not normal for them to live longer lives. God did not design misfits to stick around in His perfect society. He expected their quick demise."

"I know they're going to die. I'm simply trying to slow the process down; same as I'd do for you if you were hurting. Them having a flaw here or a missing limb there, simply means they need me more."

"Christmas needs you more."

"I can't be responsible for the shortsightedness of your worker elves when it comes to meeting the needs of those less fortunate in life. It's not me. I got to be me; point blank."

Nicholas said, "Slowing down the process for those animals closest to you is understandable. We think of them as family, as pets; like my reindeer. But slowing it down for every tom, dick and hairy deer that comes up the dusty road is ridiculous; and expensive."

"It's worth it."

"Think so? I don't. It is neither cost-effective nor a good use of our limited resources, to try to save the life of every cripple. It's also a poor use of your time. Bottom line efficiency goes right out the window; as quick as melted snow."

"I love these animals, Nick. I don't see how I can do what you want. It goes against everything I believe."

"What you can do is to change the image folks get when they see how you treat them. Change the image, and it'll change their minds about you."

Franken's brows rose with interest.

"Change the image? How so?"

Santa Nicholas sat up straight and shifted his weight to the couch's edge.

Here was his chance to set the record straight, like the Elders had told him to do.

"Well, take your title for example. Like you say, you're a certified vet but you're also a duly licensed medical practitioner. Yet, you advertise yourself as a veterinary doctor but rarely mention your medical practice. You prioritize your animals first."

"Working with animals is my passion. Working with malformed elves is a necessity. Some medical doctors refuse to see crippled children altogether, putting them at the end of the line when it comes to their care; hoping they will just fade away before they get to the front of the line."

"Don't you see it, Franken Jack? That's normal treatment for misfits. We breed up, not down. You've branded yourself as favoring deformed creatures over normal ones. We need to change the image of the brand."

"I have never had a problem with my brand; thank you."

"No man is an island in Clausdom. Islands are like a pimple which eventually comes to a head and pops. Kind of like what happened with our brother Bourbon. He popped right on out of here to the TOR region, as soon as his sins rose to the surface."

"You're doing it again; you're actually comparing me and my dinos to Bourbon and his lust-filled elves."

"It isn't me so much as it is those I represent as Santa. Clausdom folks like traditional normalcy. It's what God intended. Folks like bettering themselves in life. When they see birth blunders in public, they try to fix the image. That is being normal."

"You know, Nick," Doctor Franken said, "Folks have to stoop pretty low to consider dinos as mistakes in God's creation. And for you to compare me to Bourbon's activities a second time in one Red House meeting, well, it is downright unfriendly."

"I meant it only as an analogy; I meant nothing personal by it."

"Bourbon's ideas and activities hurt others. Worse yet, his morals are almost nonexistent. He sleeps with men; he sleeps with women, and he sleeps with animals. Me now, I'm an oath-sworn Doctor. I've always tried to help anyone and everyone; the healthy and the hurting."

"I'm afraid I'm at a loss for words. I just can't get it through that thick head of yours, how your treating disabled animals in such a high manner is offending the citizens of Clausdom. That's the whole point of this conversation."

"I'm only trying to take care of those who need a helping hand. Are we about done here? This is getting old, and I am not getting any younger."

The room went quiet.

His Santa brother said nothing; just stood there and stared at the Santa pictures on the wall.

FRANKEN JACK CLAUS sat down on the edge of the sofa chair he'd claimed as his.

It was difficult for him to understand the shortsightedness of such a closed mind, when it came to lending a helping hand to those less fortunate.

He answered his brother's stoic silence with frustration, "Nicholas Henry Claus, do you hear what you're saying? You're Santa Claus, for Heaven's sake. You should record yourself speaking sometime, and then listen to it afterwards."

When Santa Nicholas heard the word 'recording,' he gulped hard; sitting up sharply like he'd just been stabbed in the back.

He wondered if his brother knew his very words were being secretly recorded, even as he spoke.

Nicholas listened closer to his brother's words.

"You're supposed to be Santa-for-one, Santa-for-all. Don't leave my dinos behind, I beseech you. They deserve your mercy."

His concern about hidden recording laid to rest, Nicholas said, "Look, Franken, I'm just saying if you worked on the more perfect animals twice as much as the handicapped ones, those unclean ones you care about so much wouldn't come into Clausdom conversations so much."

"Well, sorry Charlie, I can't do that. It's misleading to deceive others of my honest intentions."

"So what if it's misleading? If it misleads Clausdom folks into feeling better, who cares? If a little deception gets you off the hook, who cares? I don't. And I'm Santa!"

"I care," Franken said. "I have to live with myself. I won't lie to others or to myself."

"There it is, Franken; there's the root of the ruckus. Your stinking pride always comes into play when we talk. You care more about helping these unclean animals than about supporting the boys and girls at Christmastime. With you, the Christmas gift-run takes second place. You're a Claus. Act like one."

"I know I'm a Claus. But I'm doing my level best to honor the name and stay true to my heart's desires at the same time. I'm more than just a name or a title."

"Folks here in Clausdom got eyes, Franken. They're not stupid. A man's actions define who he is. A man's works follow his faith. Elves see how you care more for your dinos than you do them. They resent it; especially the fact you're doing nothing to help them meet their Christmas quotas each month."

Franken said, "In my heart, I care for them both equally. I try to be fair and balanced. If your worker elves have issues with my decisions, that's on them."

"Don't you see it? Animal dinos aren't even close to being equal to unblemished humans. You have no right to feel as intense about helping unfit animals as you do humans. It's wrong."

"Maybe it's you that's wrong; did you bother to consider that possibility?"

Nicholas brushed off the suggestion.

"I'm not alone in this. The Elders are on my side. And most toyshop workers resent your radical beliefs; chiefly the fact you're doing nothing to help them meet their quotas each month."

"You're talking shop quotas with me? Really? "

"Yes, I am," Nicholas said. "Look at the big picture, Franken. Rising quotas and orders not filled in time, force workers to spend more time away from their families. It's lost time, for which they now blame you."

"Well, I can't do much there. Their work; their quotas. Your job, your problem. Leave me out of it."

"This is the North Pole, Mister Claus," Nicholas chided; slipping his demeanor into official Santa mode at this time.

Standing up, Santa Nick kicked out his legs outward to remove the kinks.

He found himself becoming increasingly agitated the more his brother defended Clausdom's dino element.

The end of this conversation couldn't come none too soon for him.

He went on speaking, though, as was his duty.

Interestingly enough, he was oblivious his words now had a razor sharp edge developing across their tone.

Franken asked, "So this is the North Pole? So what?"

"So, every resident has an obligation to help out with Christmas gifts; making them, boxing them or wrapping them. You're shirking your duties and I've always let it pass because of you being family. I can't do that no more. The High Court is involved; it's out of my hands now."

It was becoming obvious to Doctor Franken how his Santa brother was under notable duress.

His voice had changed. Beads of sweat were bursting beneath his hairline.

Feeling sorry for his kin, Franken therefore relented.

"Look, Nick, if you're that bad off, I'll agree to do what I can for Christmas with what little spare time I have."

"It's not enough."

"It'll have to be. Your workshops turning into sweat workshops is not my primary responsibility; it's yours. Deal with it. Use all those extraordinary Santa powers the Twenty-Four Elders gave you and not me. You're the reigning Santa, aren't you? I'm older, but you got appointed Santa. And I think we both know why."

"Back to that again, are we? So, I'm Santa; so what?"

"So, if the Elders had chosen me instead of you, we wouldn't be having this conversation. I'd bite down hard on the reins and get the job done. You sure wouldn't find me whining over melted snow."

"Folks are demanding change, Franken."

"Lest I repeat myself, I told you I'd try to help more. But you have to accept the fact I haven't been given Ownership of the Christmas gift-run. If the Elders had chosen me instead of you as Santa, it would be my top priority, and we wouldn't be having this conversation. Unlike you, I would have already resolved the situation."

"Your attitude leaves much to be desired, Brother Franken. You're backing me into a corner with the way the worker elves feel about you; not to mention a certain Twenty-Four Elders."

"Folks who want what others have are always whining about something; mostly out of jealousy. And don't worry about me, Nicholas Henry. I can stand the heat. It's not like I just got this facial birthmark overnight. I've lived with people making fun of it and me my whole life."

"I think we can leave your birthmark out of this. You might be able to shrug this dino matter off by making light of it, but I can't. Clausdom workers are upset to the boiling point. I'm going to have a mutiny on my hands if I'm not careful."

"Look at it this way, brother Santa. If their snot-nosed buzzing wasn't about me, it'd be about someone else. Maybe even you. You should thank me, it's me; and leave me extra gifts come Christmas morning. You owe me."

"I owe you all right. And when the snow in the dead of winter melts, you can expect payment. But for now, what say we not resurrect any more gunnysack memories involving that birthmark of yours from our past. I've never cared for discussing it."

"Fine by me; I have memories I'd like to forget. Unfortunately, the worst of them memories like to hang on like vultures."

"So?" Nicholas said. "Deal with it."

"I'm trying."

"Try harder."

A Frankenclaus Book!

8
WHEN FAMILY MEMBERS WAR!

SANTA NICHOLAS chose that moment to open the side doors to his office.

Stepping into the hallway, he almost ran smack-dab into a maid. He excused himself and she went on. Only then did he feel his muscles lose their tension from the heated conversation inside his office.

He needed a bit of fresh air, if he was to distance himself from the problem at hand and in so doing, have a clear head for what the Elders had ordered him to do if his brother failed to listen to reason.

Staring at a hallway empty of activity, Nicholas wondered if he really did owe his brother a debt of gratitude, as his older brother had implied.

Standing under the arch as deaf and dumb as one of his brother's patients, Santa Nicholas stared both ways down the hallway, looking for answers he knew wouldn't come.

His older outlier brother, one Franken Jack Claus, was bringing Nicholas to the pinnacle of frustration; forcing him to search out a spot of freshness as a way of surviving the staleness within.

Leaving the doors open, he turned to see his brother walking over to the pull-cord for the second time.

"Blast it," Nicholas muttered to himself. "Would the man ever learn this wasn't his house?"

Franken asked, "You want me to pull the cord again?"

"No, I don't. Give them ten more minutes," Nicholas said. "Something must be holding them up in the kitchen. Sarah knows you're here. She'll hurry them along."

"Ten minutes it is, then. I'd like a Clausdo or two before I go."

NICHOLAS LOOKED CLOSELY at his brother's profile which was sideways to him.

The grotesque birthmark was being enhanced by the reflection of the light from its surface. Nicholas paused; taking a split second to ponder over if he was really going to say what he was going to say.

"Franken? Do you know folks call you Doctor Frankenclaus behind your back; after that Frankenstein creature in the movies?"

Franken Jack Claus chuckled. "I've heard the scuttlebutt. I don't pay it much mind."

"Well, I do," Nicholas said; walking further into the room. "They're comparing your personality with that medieval monster's. You see what's happening, don't you? They're laughing at you behind your back; like when we were kids. It's embarrassing and worse yet, I'm at a loss as to how to stop it."

"Well, Brother Nick, that being said, I appreciate the concern. Personally, I see three things here."

"Three?"

"Three. First off, I am indeed a doctor and on two counts at that. And if you run my names together, Frankenclaus is my name in a sense. And even you, as Santa Claus, must admit there's no getting around the purplish mark covering half my face."

"It's not covering half your face; only the cheek."

"And part of the upper neck as well."

"That's not noticeable, so it doesn't count. And as far as I'm concerned, I've known you since I was born. So, I don't really see the blotch as being anything but normal on you."

"Children and those adults with weak stomachs don't see it that way. To them, my maroon blotch is monstrous in appearance; hideous in fact when it's on a Claus son. And most especially revolting when compared to handsome faces such as your son, Junior has."

"No objections there, Junior is a fine cut of a young man; a chip off the old block."

"He is. So, compared to his extreme handsomeness, it's only natural for regular folks to feel awkward in my presence. Time and again when they think I'm not looking, I catch them staring at my disfigurement. I try to let it go, but it does get rather annoying when it happens so often."

"I suspect that's true enough. I'm sorry."

"Worse yet, when they're trying to look me straight in the face to talk to me, I can see the personal struggle in their eyes as they fight to turn a blind eye to the Lord's purple brand He's put on my life."

Seeing Nicholas Henry turn a sharp eye to look at him closely, Franken Jack said, "Don't worry, Santa, I'm not trying to curse God and die. You don't have to send for the men in the white coats just yet."

"You sure? I don't like the way you're talking."

"Don't take it personal; I don't. It's not like I can hide what's in plain sight for the world to see."

"You shouldn't put yourself down like that just because of a birthmark. It'll lead to clinical depression, and that would only compound the shame of having a blemish."

"I don't mind talking about my face. Sometimes, it even scares me when I look in the mirror of a morning." Franken chuckled, rubbing the right side of his cheek to feel the butt of his funny.

"That's just a birthmark you got there, though," Nicholas said. "It has nothing to do with that Frankenstein monster of Mary Shelly's. Folks have no right to line you up with him."

"Maybe it's a gift they're giving me."

"A gift, really? Don't make light of what I'm saying, Franken. I'm serious. Aren't you offended the least bit how certain loose mouths are deriding the Claus name because of Shelly's creature?"

"I could be offended, I suppose; if I was the type of man to take offense; which I'm not."

Nicholas said, "When it comes to a person's name, you should take offense when folks make fun of it. It's downright disrespectful. A man's name is who he is. If he has no name, he has no honor."

"Being offended, Brother Nicholas, involves allowing far too many negative emotions to take control of a person. It's not worth it. I learned that the hard way. Besides, tending to the physical and emotional needs of my patients doesn't leave me much time for outside interests."

Nicholas snapped, "If you don't pay attention to outside interests, they'll surely pay attention to you."

"Apparently so, if what you're telling me is the truth."

"Santa doesn't lie."

"No, but Santa sure fudges. Nothing much changes in Clausdom, does it,

Brother? It is the same as when we were kids. Clausdom proper is the perfect society; created for perfect people with perfect animals. I didn't like the idea then; it's even less appealing to me now."

"Correction. It used to be the perfect," Nick said, returning to the sofa. "Circumstances are different now."

"If you're talking about me in particular, I've lived with this blemish all my life. So, if folks are making fun of me and it bothers you, tell them to stop. You're the reigning Santa. I should have been, of course, but they didn't want me. They wanted someone who didn't have my face."

"Still sore about that, are we? Well, that's too bad. Grow up," Nick snarled. "What's at stake here is your reputation as a Claus, not how pretty you look. The voices of a liberal few have spawned a movement against you. It's escalating."

"There's got to be more to this than just me, Nicholas Henry. I'm small fish compared to the sharks in these firmament waters of yours."

"The real sharks, dear Brother, are all south of the tundra. The world's population is squeezing our resources dry. Haven't you been listening to what I've been saying?"

"I know Earth's population has been increasing at an alarming rate since the turn of the century. I'm not totally blind to current events. I work with shut-ins; I'm not shut-in myself."

Nicholas said, "Well, it's all going to come to a head someday; you mark my word. There will be a mass shortage of global resources, and not just ours. Riots will occur. People will die. In some parts of the world, even now, the weather is turning against us."

"Isn't that the world's problem; not ours?"

"Not ours? Not ours?" Nick's head jerked around, his chest heaving outward. "It's become ours, Mister. It's like falling dominos."

"What is like falling dominos? Having more babies?"

"Hello? More babies mean more people. More people mean more children. More children mean more gifts. More gifts mean the same number of folks in Clausdom have to work three times as hard to meet the rising quotas for Christmas Eve's gift-run."

"You put it that way; it sounds rough, all right."

"Workers have little family time. Their frustration has come to a boiling point you're the release valve."

"Seems to me, Mister Santa, folks need to start their own, baby domino movement here in Clausdom. Maybe you should let all these workers go home for lunch once a week as a fringe benefit. You know; to perfect the art of procreation."

"Huh? You mean..." Santa Nick's eyebrows arched skyward.

NICHOLAS' REACTION to such words didn't surprise Franken. His brother had always been a bit conservative in that department. He continued his line of thought.

"Look at it this way, Nick; reproducing more Clausdom children would mean more workers for the toy shops. More workers would mean fewer hours worked per person; which would then translate into more family time for everyone."

"And you? What about you when it comes to having a son? Are you going to just sit idly by and watch; same as always? In case you haven't noticed, we could use another Claus son as an apprentice to my Junior."

"Forget about me," Franken said, cushioning his stout behind on one of the bar counter's stools. "We don't need another Frankenstein around here."

"Please don't talk like that. Just because you came out marked, doesn't mean your son will."

"Whatever you say, Mister Santa Claus. Nevertheless, birthing more babies is still the real key to solving your pressure cooker problem. The root problem is you're short on manpower. You're Santa. Order people to have sex without safety. It'll be fun for everyone."

"It doesn't solve the problem of folks taking the name of a Claus in vain because of you. The Twenty-Four Elders believe if citizens are mocking a Claus, they're mocking the entire, ancestral Santa lineage. They want something done about it."

Franken sneered. "Yeah, I see it now. Here it comes. The truth finally comes creepy crawling its way out of the shadows."

"Don't get riled up; not when I'm trying to talk sensible to you."

"Everything always comes back to what the Elders have decided, doesn't it? Well, Nicholas Henry Claus, the way I see it, in making light of me and not you, at least folks are doing something they enjoy. I make them happy."

"Where in thunder is your pride in being a Claus, for Christmas sake? They're saying in effect your Claus name is worthless."

"My pride is in taking care of those ill-suited for this life. I wouldn't get too worked up over a little name change. It's best to forgive and forget. Life is short. If it doesn't bother me, it shouldn't bother you."

Santa Nicholas raised his voice. "Folks are disrespectful of you as a Claus. Get upset. Do something. Pick up a chair and throw it across the room. Show some backbone instead of being such a sissy."

"I'm not the sissy; Brother Bourbon is."

"Don't try to escape the conversation by bringing him up. Try to stay on-task for once. I'm speaking as the official Clausdom Santa."

"Fine; have it your way. For my part, Mister Official Clausdom Santa, I see no reason to either encourage or discourage name-callers. Folks grow into maturity at different rates. Let them do what they will. I don't intend to stop them, much less defend where I set my own, personal priorities in life. We're to turn the other cheek, remember?"

"That's not funny."

"Wasn't meant to be," Franken said with a dogged demeanor.

"Well, Mister Smarty-Pants, the High Court is not so willing to turn the other cheek this time. The Twenty-Four Elders put me on notice. They want something done officially. They're demanding action be taken to resolve the matter."

"So, the Elders want action taken against me, do they?"

"It's not so much against you, as it is against your dino disasters. If this labor scandal gets into the History Annals, the Elders say it will be a blight on their watch as well as mine."

"So, the bottom line finally oozes out of the turnip, does it? I suspected something like this would come down the slippery Elder slope some day. But it never occurred to me I'd be blindsided by a member of my own family."

SANTA NICHOLAS CLAUS remained mute at the verbal swipe of his older brother.

And Franken Jack Claus knew why.

After all, what could Nicholas say in his own defense? Nothing of any consequence, for sure.

What had been said by him was true.

Santa Claus always took the side of the Twenty-Four Elders of the High Court of Clausdom. It came with the title.

A Frankenclaus Book!

9
THE FIRST SHOE DROPS

TO DOCTOR FRANKEN, this brotherly meeting had gone on much longer than he'd planned. He had a baby calf with missing front legs to get back to, and all this talk about Santa Claus wanting her put down was nauseating.

Franken Jack fidgeted nervously, shuffling his tall form around the room for the second time in what was but a handful of minutes. In his mind, he went over everything the younger Nicholas had said.

From time to time when his feathers got ruffled at being boxed in by Santa furniture, he simply meandered around in circles, all the while murmuring to himself fitfully.

His Santa brother finally broke the silence, which had become embarrassing for both of them.

"I can't understand you," Nicholas ushered out. "Speak up those thoughts of yours so I can hear you."

"I was only reminding myself how all my life, everything always comes back to what twenty-four men decide is best for me. I knew there was a rat in the woodpile the minute you said the workers were being pushed to meet increased quotas."

"And?"

"And we both know only the Elders can raise quotas to exorbitant levels. Now, because they did so and the workers don't like it, complaints had been submitted to the High Court. It's not the workers who are upset with me; it's those Twenty-Four Elders. If they lowered the quotas, it would solve everything."

"If they lowered the quotas, some boys and girls would not receive gifts on Christmas morning. Let's get one thing straight here, Franken. I have to work these folks hard. I've no choice."

"Everyone has a choice. You could make smaller gifts or give out fewer gifts to each person."

"The right amount of gifts has to be made each month. Gifts not made can't be delivered. As far as the workers go, they only want you to pitch in and help ease their workload by using your Claus superpowers. Is that so wrong?"

"If it really is the workers complaining in my case, yes; it is wrong."

"Why is it wrong? You can do ten times as much as any two of them on any given day. You may not have the Santa anointing, but you do have the Claus anointing. They don't have either. They're worker bees."

"I'd like to help you, Brother Nick; but I can't. Like I said, I have no spare time to do more than take a snow-bath and grab a bite to eat. If it weren't for young Frankie helping me out from time to time, I don't know what I'd do."

"That's your story? That's your final word?"

"My final word and I'm sticking to it."

Doctor Franken's lips went wide at his funny; making the birthmark on his puffed-up cheek turn a deep purple.

His Santa brother was trying to rile him; to goad him into doing something that went against the grain of his faith. He would have none of it.

"I was afraid you'd say that," Nick said.

"No matter what you say, little Santa brother, I'm not going to get all riled up over workshop workloads, the global population explosion or climate change messing up the weather. And that's final."

"I'm sorry to hear that," Nicholas said.

"And if more folks nickname me after Miss Mary's Frankenstein creature, so be it. They're calling my dinos far worse. At least with me and my complexion, it's an easy transition."

"It's disappointing to hear you say that; mighty disappointing. A man's image is all he has in the way of honor."

"I can't very well change my face, Nicholas; had it too long," Franken smiled. He leisurely crossed his legs, swinging his loose foot wildly as he let the wit of his words sink in.

He had been in control of his life when he'd entered the study, and he fully intended to keep it that way until he left the study. That being said, he did love his Santa brother; so he was doing his level best to exercise medicinal patience at his brother's obviously growing anxiety.

His little brother didn't know it, but the tenseness in his brow had become increasingly worse the longer the two disagreed. The fact Santa's blood pressure was on the rise was all too apparent.

Nicholas' tone was firm, "I'm not talking about your face, Franken Jack." He slapped his red, velvet Santa trousers. "Neither are the Elders. You're a Claus. The Elders accept you as a Claus, for better or for worse."

"But?"

"But those malformed dino animals you care for are different. They don't belong here in Clausdom."

"My dino animals are different, you say, than me and my face? I don't see how. Some flaws are able to be seen, like mine. Others like yours, Brother Santa, are hidden away on the inside; buried deep within the soul."

"Stop trying to justify imperfection."

"We all have disfigurements at some level, Santa Nick. Yours just happen to be spiritual. Or you wouldn't be trying to push this agenda of the Elders off on me."

"The fact you were born a Claus makes you several notches above them dino creatures of yours in intelligence. Most of them are idiots or morons, from what I understand."

Franken could do naught but glare by way of response. It had been a long time since he'd sat still and let anyone criticize his animals so. He felt like walking out. But that would be disrespectful of a Santa. And showing disrespect would be a Naughty thing to do.

His thoughts were interrupted by a loud knock, knock, knock on the solid oak wood of the double doors leading into the office area.

DELORES TULIP entered the room, pot in hand. She was followed by Miss Daisy Delight, who was carrying a small tray stacked high with Clausdo doughnuts; each one glazed over with tiny flakes of crusty honey-bee sweetener, and center-filled with a tablespoon of frozen ice cream.

Miss Tulip spoke first. "Here is your hot chocolate, Mister Santa Nicholas, sir. Miss Sarah added in the marshmallows. I'll pour you a cup if you like."

"Yes, please do. Hot chocolate always tastes better with marshmallows."

Miss Daisy looked towards Santa's older brother. "And Mister Franken, sir, here are your Clausdos; as ordered. They are from Miss Sarah. She sends her regards. I'll set them here on the counter."

Having stood up to receive the ladies, Santa Nicholas said, "Miss Tulip, I'll have you know hot chocolate is exactly what I need right now. Thank you, young lady; and you, too, Miss Daisy. You can set mine down on the end table. I'll let it cool a bit."

Franken walked across the room to Miss Daisy; declaring without hesitation, "I'll take that tray of doughnuts, Miss Daisy. I'm ravishingly hungry. What in snow took you two so long? You have to go clear to the South Pole to get these doughnuts?"

"No, sir," Miss Daisy replied. "Miss Sarah wouldn't let us bring you the older ones from yesterday's batch like we wanted. She made these fresh; just for you."

"In that case, you can give her my warmest thanks. We'll be keeping this tray. I'd hate to disappoint Miss Sarah by not eating at least half of these doughnuts. The way I feel, I could eat a polar bear all by myself."

Nicholas Claus softened his brother's words. "Don't mind my brother, Miss Daisy. He's used to working with animals with attitudes. You two can leave now."

"Yes, Santa Nicholas, sir. If you need anything else, just pull the rope. One of us will be here at the earliest."

"Fine; now, please close the door on your way out. Your efforts on our behalf have been Nice."

"Thank you, Santa. We'll thank Miss Sarah for you, Mister Franken, sir."

Franken chomped down on a Clausdo as a bear on a bone, speaking with his mouth half full as a spot of melting ice cream drooled from the sides of his mouth. "Do that. Thank her for me, too. These are delicious Clausdos, girls. Give my compliments to the kitchen staff."

"Yes, sir; good day." Miss Tulip nodded politely as she backed out of the room. It was considered disrespectful for a maid to turn her back on a reigning Santa in Santa's own house.

NICHOLAS CLAUS observed the two ladies move towards the hallway. He resolved to bring the conversation with his brother to its fateful conclusion; openly revealing what the Twenty-Four Elders had sent him to tell his blemished brother.

He'd already said the brunt of what he had to say to try to get his brother out of being nailed to the Cross. Franken had rebuffed his every suggestion.

All that was left now was to inform his brother of the fallout from the Elders, of what was decreed to be done to all of Clausdom's deformed dinos.

Following Miss Daisy and Miss Delores to the double doors, Nicholas made certain to close those doors securely once they'd passed through; lest they pause and accidently hear things they shouldn't in his conversation with his brother.

As he heard the dull click of the twin doors fastening together, he was mentally prepping himself to bring his tête-à-tête with his brother to some sort of agreed-upon solution to what the Elders had proposed.

By the time Nicholas' mind was set and he had swiveled around on his heels to implement his decisions, he took note of the fact Franken had sequestered the entire tray brimming with doughnuts.

He'd already moved them closer to the chair he had previously pulled out for himself.

Some things never changed, Santa Nick was thinking. His brother had not only chosen the largest donut on the tray to eat first, but the one with the most ice cream filling.

Not to be outdone, Nicholas boldly walked over and picked up what amounted to the second largest Clausdo from the tray; it had much less ice cream than Franken's, but considerably more honey flakes.

At the same time, Santa Nick nonchalantly picked up the tray and placed it on a side table, more or less median betwixt the two of them. It was a bold move, but one he felt was necessary to establish the fact he was the Santa, and this was this house.

Holding up his doughnut while giving his brother an accusing glance, Nicholas said, "Don't mind if I have at least one of these Clausdos, do you?"

"Not at all, Mister Santa," Franken smiled a guilty look of confession. "Have two even.

We can always order up a second tray if these aren't enough. You and I both know Sarah never makes just one tray of Clausdos. The house staff would never forgive her."

Turning away, Nicholas went to the end table where his cup of hot chocolate had cooled down. He realized there was no easy way he could tell his brother what conclusions the Elders had arrived at, much less what they had subsequently given him to say out of his official capacity as Santa Claus.

Dipping his Clausdo into the steaming cup of hot chocolate, Nicholas Henry thought about his facially disfigured brother's personality, and how he had reacted to bad news when they were growing up together.

It was then he came to the abrupt conclusion on how for his brother, at least, it was best to use a sharp knife on the issue at hand and make the cut clean. Get it out and get it over with; that was his wrapping-up-the-moment idea.

So, having the outline of a tentative game plan, he jumped into the cold waters of contention.

"Look, Franken, I know this has been a long night and I don't want to drag this thing out any further."

"It's about time you made up your mind on that. The conversation we've had tonight, pretty much sums up conversations we've had in the past. Neither of us change what we believe."

"Tonight, Franken, is a turning point. It's one thing you setting up orphan homes to take in handicapped children whose parents have either died or no longer have the wherewithal to deal with the disabled child's day-to-day needs. This is only to be expected of those more fortunate in life. "

"I do have my reasons. Even the disabled deserve having a doctor who cares."

"And Clausdom folks understand your reasons for helping them and accept them."

"As they should," Franken said; in betwixt healthy bites of his second Clausdo. "These are really good this time."

Santa Nicholas went on, "It's only reasonable to see you care for the marred ones because you've got a birthmark flaw as well; same as them. So, it's only natural you'd want to help others in the same boat."

"Spoken like the opening statement of an impeccable lawyer in a narrow-minded courtroom. So, what's the High Court punch line, Nicholas? It doesn't take an Elder to see you're sucking on a polar stone. This isn't my first sleigh ride, you know."

"I'm trying to get this out the right way; to make what I have to say white as snow. I'm not sure I can."

"Just spit the bottom line out first, Brother Santa. We're both adults. You can't hide the fact you're on a secret mission from the Twenty-Four Elders. I've been here before. If you need more courage, grab another Clausdo. It works for me."

"Franken? As far as the Elders are concerned, carrying your special needs philosophy over from children to animals makes for a warped ideology to live by. Its very nature isolates everyone else's needs so they come up short. It's unbecoming a Claus."

"I disagree. I consider all those who have no such compassion as warped in principle."

"Clausdom has always believed animals born with severe abnormalities had to be put down. It is neither cost-effective nor time-efficient to tend to them. The bottom line here is the High Court believes it best for us to return to our traditional roots."

"I'm well aware of tundra tradition for four-legged invalids, Nicholas Henry," Franken Jack arched his back smartly. His shoulders became stiff when he thrust his chin forward. "I used to have nightmares over it when I was a boy."

"You shouldn't have. The most merciful thing a person can do for a dino misfit is to take the deformed creature far out into the tundra and leave him. Let him die a quick and painless death in the freezing cold. That's what our forefathers believed, and it's written in the Annals of Clausdom."

"It's not what I believe."

"If it was good enough for them, Mister, it should be good enough for me and you. We're their descendants, are we not?"

"I know what went on before, Nicholas Henry. Thank God we've stopped being so barbaric."

"I wouldn't be thanking God too soon, Franken. I was hoping you'd accept my invite today. I was also hoping we'd be able to discuss the animal problem reasonably as men first. As brothers, we'd then come up with a solution we could all agree on; you, me and the Elders."

"My solution, Mister Nicholas Santa, is for them busybody Elders to back off and leave well enough alone. Me and mine are doing just fine without their meddling in and muddying the pot."

"I give up," Nicholas threw up his hands; reckoning it was time to drop the hammer. He took two steps towards his brother, who had in turn taken up residence on a stool adjacent to the doughnuts.

"Here it is, Mister Franken Jack Claus," Nick declared officially. "If you're refusing to toe the line as a Claus when it comes to supporting Christmas, the Elders have elected to mandate certain actions be implemented against all dinos; animals and human alike."

"I thought you said the disabled children weren't part of this evening's discussion."

"They weren't. They are now, and only because you refuse to submit to Clausdom protocol."

"I can't say I like the sound of that," Franken said derogatorily. "Aren't you supposed to be Nice, Mister Santa Claus? Maybe Brother Bourbon was right about you and the High Court being too pompous and overbearing."

"I'm warning you, Franken Jack, you'd best work with me on this," Nicholas said; taking two more steps towards his brother to emphasize his dominant position.

"Spit the rest of it out, Nicholas Henry. Any fool can see you're holding something back," Franken chastised viciously; lower lip quivering as the upper one froze stiff. How dare they attack his disabled kids! They were just children.

DOCTOR FRANKEN CLAUS didn't like being threatened any more than his twin brother, Bourbon Tor Claus; who had moved out of Clausdom to the mining region of TOR because of it.

He now lived in ice caves; where he and his followers spent their days mining precious stones and their nights getting preciously stoned; not to mention his sinning in wild, unmentionable ways with a multitude of his citizens.

Standing up, Franken imitated his brother; moving forward in turn. He threw a knee atop the closest sofa chair's armrest. "Can't talk, Nicholas? If you're hard of hearing, maybe you should see a real doctor; one who can grow a longer beard and whose hair is not thinning so badly in the back."

Santa Nicholas heaved a heavy sigh. "You just don't get it, do you? You've gone and crossed the line and you don't even know how far. I'm not hard of hearing; but you sure seem to be hard of listening. There's a storm brewing and you can't even feel the chills."

Nicholas began a slow walk about the room. He intentionally formed sharp circles around where his brother was standing; so as to intimidate him about what was to be told him from the Twenty-Four Elders.

"Franken?" Nicholas said. "The Elders have declared all misshapen dino animals are to be removed from Clausdom forthwith. They are to be sent to the Neitherland region or the tundra, depending on the seriousness of their condition. It is the Elders' intention to make Clausdom a perfect society in all its ways."

"Excuse me?" Franken exclaimed, abruptly coming erect. For the second time in two minutes, he was in shock. First his dino children were being attacked, and now his dino animals. It was surreal; absurd beyond anything he imagined.

He fought to control the fury rising up within him. His shoulders once again arched back in synchronous motion to his chin being thrust upwards.

"The worse ones will go to the tundra, of course. Their death will be swift and merciful, as per God's perfect will. Of those going to Neitherland, all will be given a chance but it is expected only the strongest will survive. And of those that do, they'll have to move further south to stay alive."

"You mean they'll have to distance themselves from Clausdom, isn't that it?"

"Satisfied? You made me say it. I didn't want to. But you and your thick head made me do it anyway."

"You can't be serious, Nick. What you're suggesting is crazy. Why my dinos? Why now?"

"Like you said, you have no spare time to help in the workshops where Claus descendants belong. The Twenty-Four Elders understand your problem and the dilemma you're in. So they're making it so you have all the time in the world to better serve our Christmas gift-giving activities."

"But, why bring the tundra into this? It's going too far; even for the Elders. And as for the Neitherland region, it's hardly survivable by humans, much less by animals with impairments. Most of them will die if they don't get help. And it won't be merciful. They'll suffer when they go."

"Forget the animals, Franken. Animals are animals. They come. They go. Let's talk people. Doesn't it bother you when your friends and family have such a low opinion of you as a person? You should try to think of someone besides yourself for a change; stop being so selfish."

FRANKEN was speechless.

The High Court had crossed the line of no return as far as he was concerned.

He wasn't sure what he was going to do, but do something he would in due time; just as soon as the aggressive thoughts in his mind settled down, so he could think clearly enough to make a sound decision.

"Nicholas Henry," he said, measuring out his words slowly and carefully, "the Twenty-Four Elders are looking at this all wrong."

"How so?"

"Low opinions of others come about because when folks look in the mirror, they don't like what they see through the windows of their own eyes. The true feelings of these complaining workers have nothing to do with me at all."

Nicholas responded. "Nevertheless, it's been decided you're a distraction that's negatively affecting Clausdom workers. You've saved so many of these dinos from dying, my workers are spending more time talking about you than they are working. That's got to stop."

"I don't see how it can. I'm certainly not going to kill the animals I love. I'm a doctor, for Christmas sake."

"If you're willing to change, maybe I can put in a good word for you with the Elders, and let you keep a couple of them critters as indoor pets."

"I said it once and I'll say it again; my time is my time; my animals are my animals. What you and your workers do with your time is none of my concern."

"It should too be your concern. I thought I'd made that much plain."

"Santa, and right now I'm using that name loosely, I am the physician of all who are handicapped, human and animal alike. It's what I do. What else did the Elders say about my dinos; the ones who can't defend themselves?"

"I'm trying to help you, Brother Franken, if you'll listen. There's a bit of wiggle room here for you to continue to work with disabled children, but let the Elders dump the dino animals like in the old days. Stop trying to save them."

"You don't know what you're saying. I have no choice but to save them. It's who I am."

"I think I can convince the Elders to let them die out by attrition, if you're willing to stop trying to save them at birth. Work with me on this. It'll take longer to finish them off and give you time to adjust. The Elders might just accept that as a solution, as long as you're using your Claus Anointing in the workshops."

"No offense, Santa, but I'm getting tired of hearing what the Elders want."

"What they want is for you to do the right thing. To be blunt, we breed up; not down; period."

"I can't go there. If I have to choose between dedicating my life to helping

147

handicapped children or deformed animals, I choose the animals. They need me more. Most Clausdom doctors will eventually help a disabled child out of mercy. The only thing they'll do with a deformed animal is put it down."

"Christmas hogwash, Mister; the fact you're a member of the Claus Clan supersedes all else. Serving Christmas is more important than serving dinodeer or any other bush league animals."

"Not to me. Not when I'm not the duly appointed Santa."

"Why are you being so bullheaded? Can't you see I'm in a fix here? I'm caught like a punching bag between you, the Elders and tradition."

FRANKEN didn't answer right off.

Instead, he sat down in his sofa chair, and took a deep, melancholy breath before answering his brother's retort.

His body was telling him he'd eaten one too many doughnuts on an empty stomach. He shouldn't have, but he couldn't resist. He was hungry.

Now, all he really wanted to do was to go somewhere and lie down. Sad as it was, sometimes his fleshly desires got the better of his common sense. He'd soon have to excuse himself soon and tend to his own needs.

As it was, from the odd high his head was experiencing, his sugar readings had most likely skyrocketed past the mile-high mark; way too high for someone who wanted to wake up the next morning alert and on his toes at first light.

Then it hit him; mental fatigue from the arguing with his brother was setting in atop a sugar high. His lips tightened; his lungs filled with air, expanding his chest to take in oxygen to its fullest extent.

Was any of this worth it, he wondered? Why not just roll over and die; give in and give up? But then, he told himself, who would take care of his animals? No one.

They'd all die without him having given his all to save them. He therefore had no choice. He had to find a way to muck himself out of the corner stall he'd been forced into.

With a hint of repentance, he said, "With Christmas being but a month away, Nicholas Henry, my helping out isn't going to make much of a difference this year. But maybe I can make some time to help. I'll try. I promise. Just don't touch my dinos."

Taking a step forward till his knee came in contact with the couch's end table, Santa Nick asked, "How soon can you try?"

"Ask the Elders to hold off on their ruling for now. I'll see what I can do to adjust my schedule and work within the system towards next year's gift-run. That's fair."

"An interesting gambit, Brother dear, and it might have worked if you'd been more compliant early on. But I'm afraid next year is too late to do you any good. The Elders have already put it to a vote. They're interested in immediate results, not untimely delays. The dye is cast; the judgment given."

"The Elders already voted on my animals? How could they do that without at least consulting me first? You talk about respect, Nicholas? They showed me no respect if they voted against a Claus without formally hearing me out."

"I agree. Unfortunately, it wasn't my call. My Santa opinion was never asked for by any of them. I'm sorry. But like I said, we might be able to turn this around and save a handful, if you're willing to work with me on a few changes."

"It's disgusting."

"Look, Franken, the best we can do now is to work within the system. I've been thinking about it. Dome Administrator Clarence tells me we're already three weeks behind making Christmas gifts, with only four weeks to go. Do the math. Workers will be doing double shifts till the First Gong sounds."

"It's the same as was done last year and the year before. You shouldn't be putting this at my feet, Nick. Who's the Santa here?"

"I am."

Frustration talking, Franken said. "Well, if you're Santa for crying out loud, then by all that's holy, be Santa. Take charge and tell those doing all the gossiping to hold their filthy tongues."

He raised his voice. "Tell the hard-of-hearing ones if they wouldn't talk so much, they could do twice as much work."

He then shouted. "Threaten to send THEM to the bloody tundra!"

Santa Nicholas let the harshness of the words fade; the room became quiet. "I don't think direct confrontation is the solution in this case, Franken."

"Yeah? Except when it comes to me, right? You tell those that gossip if they don't stop, you'll be bringing in someone else in to do their job. That's the way it is in the real world. Do the same here."

"There is no one else to bring in to do anyone's job. We're maxed out, I tell you. The Elders are expecting you to help out. We want to bring you and your Anointing in to put us over the Christmas quota."

"And if I were Santa, I surely would. But I'm not. I have a life of my own to lead. One I intend to live in the way I choose, without Elder interference. I'm sorry if it conflicts with your Santa perspective or the Elders' way of thinking. I am who I am."

"Is that your final word on this?"

"It is. Me choosing to live the way I live is not based on what your workers think of me. Nor is it based on Elder edicts being given out on a whim without due process. I have rights, don't I?"

"A man's got to consider the thoughts and opinions of others, Franken Jack. He has to live with the consequences of his beliefs. That's what makes us a cultured, educated society. Do you understand what I'm saying?"

Franken shifted sideways, turning his back to his brother so as to emphasize his next words with the full venom he intended. "I don't consider what you want to do to my animals as being either cultured or educated. It's barbaric."

"Brother dear, civilized persons toe the line when it comes to peer pressure, and functioning as one part of a larger whole in matters bigger than they are. We're both cogs in a machine."

Franken muttered, "The rotten machine can spit me out, then."

Nicholas ignored the slur. "It matters not whether we like it or not. We've no choice. We have to live with our neighbors and the Twenty-Four Elders; who make the rules of the umbrella."

"You're wrong, there, Santa Claus. I do have a choice."

"Not any longer," Nicholas moved his head from side to side. "You've been neutered and haven't even felt the pain yet. We haven't even gotten to the handicapped children yet, remember? Your trial by fire has only just begun."

"What about my crippled children?" Franken whipped around. "You're going back on your word; you know that, don't you? You promised me twice they were off-limits. Remember?"

Nicholas shook his head. "That was only if you agreed to getting rid of the animals. You didn't. Limiting the number of handicapped children in society is now back on the table. And before you ask, yes; this is straight from the Elders of the High Court of Clausdom. That makes it as official as official can get."

"But downsizing disabled children? How low can you go? You're NOT actually going to get rid of them, are you? Really, really get rid of them?"

"No, of course not; well, not exactly, anyway."

A Frankenclaus Book!

10
RIGHTEOUS WOMEN BRING PEACE

WHEN THE DOOR OPENED, both brotherly heads were startled.

In walked Sarah Claus.

Franken stood, out of courtesy and respect for his brother's wife.

"I thought I'd drop in and see how you two were getting along; fine, I hope."

She then took a closer look at their faces, as the coldness of the atmosphere hit her full force.

"Ha, ha," she smiled. "I see; not so fine. Well, to be honest, this is an old house, and some of the walls are thin. I was informed voices were being raised in here."

Nicholas Henry turned to face her, while she noted his Brother Franken had turned away.

Nicholas said, "You came at a wrong time, Sarah. Or maybe at the right time; I don't know. We're not quite done with our discussion. Perhaps you can come back later to say goodnight to Franken."

"I will leave, Santa, because it appears I'm not needed here after all. But before I go, I want to remind you two there are only two Claus sons in Clausdom of age to be Santa; you two are it. If one of you goes down, the other has to pick up the slack. It's your destiny; handed down from the earliest times when the celebration of Christmas first started."

"We know that, Sarah. What we're discussing has nothing to do with our ancestral role as keepers of the Santa Claus tradition."

Sarah went to the door and turned around.

"Good. Then you'll both be able to work together as family to resolve whatever fire it is you two are trying to put out. Always remember how we are family. And families stick together through thick and thin. I have dinner on the stove. I'll send Daisy with a couple of plates when it's done, if you like."

Franken said, "I'll pass on the offer, Sarah. Frankie's mother was born on this day, and each year Frankie makes her favorite dessert; as a way of remembering her sacrifice. I'll then tell the story of how Frankie's mother worked so hard to become pregnant. She then gave her life at the birth, so Frankie might live."

"I remember," Sarah said. "It's a sad story, but a good one Frankie must know."

"I tell it each year. With my daughter having never known her mother, this story is the only thing Frankie has to remember her by. I can't miss the dessert; so, I'll be leaving shortly."

Sarah said, "Well, if I'm still up in an hour and you're still here, I'll stop by. Otherwise, Franken, I will see you tomorrow. And you, Santa Husband, don't you be too hard on your brother. He's the only one you can rely on to back you up as Santa. And the Santa image comes before brotherly squabbles."

"Yes, my dear."

Franken said, "Thanks for stopping by, Miss Sarah. You're a pearl of a treasure in a dry and thirsty land."

Sarah peered at him; eyes narrowing. "Hmmm; let's hope the three of us are pearls when this meeting is over. Good night, you two."

Nicholas and Franken watched her go; allowing a long silence to follow in her wake.

Franken finally said, "She doesn't know what's going on here, does she?"

"She does not. It's not her place. No one knows but the Twenty-Four Elders and me; and now you."

"She's a good woman. You are blessed to have her. My Elizabeth was like that."

"Yes, she was. I'm sorry about today being her birthday. We should have had this meeting tomorrow. Now, if you'll excuse me for ten minutes, I'd like to visit the Santa facilities. My clock is ticking."

"Go for it," Franken replied. "I've got some thinking to do, anyway."

"I will be back in a bit. Help yourself to another Clausdo, if you like."

Santa Nicholas left the room with a shuffle and a shift; foretelling of what was to come one day for him in the way of a rocker.

A Frankenclaus Book!

11
THE SECOND SHOE DROPS!

FRANKEN JACK CLAUS had been dumbfounded. The startling revelation which came from the Twenty-Four Elders left him numbed.

The High Court was, in effect, changing the entire course of the activities his daily life revolved around. They were going disturb the lives of the crippled boys and girls he'd fought so hard to make happy; the ones with common and some not-so-common abnormalities.

He didn't understand all of what was happening. The Elders were deliberately attacking his special needs animals; trying to euthanize them like in the old days. That much he could understand.

It was their way to destroy animals which didn't measure up to Clausdom standards. He had stopped them before; but it looked like his string of good fortune had run its course.

The Elders considered putting dinos down as merciful. Doctor Franken, having seen quite a bit of it as a child, considered it outright murder.

Things were moving much too fast for him today. A dark cloud now lay like a pack across his spirit; making him more tired than he'd been in a long time.

Franken Jack slouched down in the sofa chair; his body sending him painful signals of the age of its own aching joints. He was too old for this, he reckoned; much too old.

He had been called to a meeting in the Red House on pretense of family fellowship. What he found was a surrogate of the High Court in the form of his Santa Claus baby brother.

His thoughts were interrupted by the return of Santa Nicholas Henry. Not waiting for his brother to talk, Franken returned to where their prior conversation had left off. He wanted to wrap things up and leave; seeing what they looked like in the morning.

"Nicholas," he said, "What you want to do to my animals is a disgrace. And changing what happiness I've brought the crippled boys and girls is unthinkable. It's an abomination. And I think Sarah will agree with me on this when she finds out. She won't like it."

"Change for the better is always difficult, Brother Claus. Change stretches a person, so more out of life can be had. You will adjust. In fact, I'm sure you will adjust; as will everyone else. The Elders are rarely wrong in their judgments."

"They're disrupting my life's passion by passing judgment on my animals. If you allow them to euthanize the odd ones, my veterinary practice in Clausdom is as good as dead."

"It's not that bad. You're a Claus son; there are many things you can do. You could, of course, help me out in the workshops. We could work side by side to meet the Christmas quotas."

Ignoring his words, Franken said, "Worse yet, you're attacking my special needs children. Why don't you just gift-wrap me for Claus Hill Cemetery? You're as much as putting me there anyway by destroying all I love."

"Don't blame me, Franken Jack. You put yourself there. Get your priorities in order; that's all we ask. Understand what's more important in the larger picture; look to the greater good for all concerned. You will be better off; Clausdom will be better off."

"I am looking to the greater good."

"Not so. Serving Christmas comes before doing good deeds to those less fortunate; even to the taking care of disabled children."

"My disabled kids are just as important to me as Christmas. They are Christmas to me, in fact; especially when I do something which makes their faces light up with joy. It's an experience well worth the effort. It's special."

Nicholas said, "We are not going to put cripples on pedestals as poster kids, Franken. It's not our way. Our traditions have always tried to make Clausdom the epitome of the perfect culture; the perfect society. We serve Christmas. Nothing is more perfect than Christmas."

"Finish it off, Nicholas Henry. Frankie's waiting on me. What else is there you're not telling me?"

"I'm getting there. This isn't easy for me either, if you must know. It's not every day a Santa has to take his own brother to task."

"I'll let that pass; as if you don't enjoy this. Go ahead, Nick; man-up. Drop the other shoe. You seem to be beating about the bush whilst being afraid to grab hold of the weeds. If you've got something else to say about my boys and girls, say it. Don't let fear and common sense hold you back."

"Fine, I'll spit it out cold if that's what you want. The Elders believe they have allowed Clausdom to move too fast in trying to keep up with the world's standards."

Franken was becoming increasing irritated by societal standards of normalcy, being used as a guillotine to cut him off from his animals and his children.

He said, "We move as the times dictate. Everyone knows that. Get to the point and cut to the chase; spit out the dinodung so we can all smell it."

"No need for vulgarity, Franken. This is the Red House, after all. If you want to swear, go down south to the Blue House or the White House. Either abounds in it just as much as misunderstanding of tradition abounds here in Clausdom."

"You can skip the Santa lecture, Nicholas."

"Don't interrupt me, please. What I have to say is important. The Elders believe Clausdom is facing problems because we've been keeping too closely aligned with the world, and not enough with tradition."

"I have nothing to do with the world."

"No, but we do. And because of this, the Elders have decided it's best if Clausdom goes back in time."

"Back in time? To what, Nick? The birth of Jesus in the manger?"

"To where the only children seen in public were perfectly formed ones; without spot or blemish. There were fewer problems with workers then. And no complaints to the High Court, I might add. The Elders believe Clausdom should return to what worked in the past."

"Well, that's flat-out demonic. It doesn't take a wizard to see that."

"No reason for spiritual sarcasm, Mister. Starting the first of the year, handicapped boys and girls are to be kept out of sight behind closed doors."

FRANKEN GASPED.

What was being done to him was unthinkable. What was to be done to his handicapped children was flat-out abuse.

"My God in Heaven. Can this get much worse? You're locking them up AGAIN?"

"They're not to be seen in public during daylight hours without a permit. And with the anticipated decrease in the use of your animal shelters, the High Court intends to make those buildings into institutions to house malformed children now being cared for in parental homes."

Franken grunted. "What are they expecting? An epidemic of more deformed births because they're sinning against my animals?"

"The Elders prefer malformed children to be separated from workers, and not be housed in normal homes as part of the family. The constant care required for them disrupts the smooth flow of the household's responsibility to Christmas."

"Really? You're taking handicapped children away from their families and putting them in institutions? That's totally insane," he railed.

Santa Nick moved closer to his brother. He sat down on the end of the coffee table directly in front of the sofa chair in which his brother was sitting. He leaned forward.

"These transitioned animal buildings will be special needs institutions, Franken; professional ones which can really help these kids. And for Christmas sake, moving these cripples is not mandatory."

"It's not?"

"No, of course not. It is, however, going to be strongly encouraged by the High Court. With their dysfunctional kids in institutions, it is expected parents will have more time to spend in the workshops, as well as being much more able to function as a normal family when at home."

"Without the burden of caring for disabled invalids around the clock, you mean?"

"Yes, of course; that's what it's all about; becoming more time-efficient in everything we do for the sake of Christmas. Don't you see? It's win-win for everyone. The crippled kids will have professional care around the clock, and normal children will have a better home life more suited to their personal needs."

"You're twisting the truth, Nicholas Henry. You're dehumanizing those who are challenged physically and mentally. I don't know how you, as the reigning Santa Claus, can sit there and tell me it's a win-win for anyone. What it is, dear brother, is a travesty."

"Better treatment for the disabled, increased family time for loved ones in the home, and more productive work being accomplished in the toyshops is a plus for you, me and them," Santa Nick decreed. "Surely even you can see that. It's not Santa Science, Franken; get real."

"I disagree, Mister."

"How so? You'll be set freed from busy work to focus your Claus Anointing more on making Christmas a success. When you're not needed in the workshops, you can help a child throw on a prosthetic arm or leg. And in your spare time, you can heal a rabid dog or clogged-up cat. It sounds fair to me; more than fair, really."

Franken uncrossed his legs and folded his arms tightly. "The Elders are wrong on this; dead wrong. Families are important. Surely as Santa, you can't be so insensitive as to do what the High Court mandates?"

"This has nothing to do with being emotionally sensible; it has everything to do with being practical and following the High Court's orders. This, as you know, is my duty as the Elder appointed Santa Claus to do."

"Don't even bring the Santa title into this, Mister. This is not the Santa Anointing I know and love. Say no more, please. We're done here."

Franken used the arms of the sofa to push himself to his feet; realizing as he did so, he shouldn't have had that last Clausdo; not when his daughter had dessert ready for him.

He asked, "When is this officially taking place, exactly?"

Santa Nicholas took to his own feet in response to his brother's aggressive move.

"It takes place the minute you walk out that door, having refused to go to work in the toyshops and leave your dino practice behind. The Elders wanted you to hear about it from me direct, not someone on the street or when it was posted. You are still a Claus; and a Claus son deserves respect."

"So, you really asked me to stop by to give me an ultimatum from them."

"As Santa, it was my job to tell you; I just didn't know how to go about it. The consensus vote was achieved by the Elders this morning. What happens now is totally up to you. You'll be making your own bed to sleep in if you refuse to toe the line. I've done all I can to soften the blow."

"First my animals, now my children. Nicholas, Nicholas, Nicholas; you sure are some Santa."

"I'm just doing my job."

"Taking baby reindeer into the wild and leaving them to die is an appalling thing for a Santa Claus to promote; even if the animals are missing a limb or two. And chaining twisted-up children to walls like what was done in the old days is an even worse disgrace. It makes me ashamed of being a Claus."

"Chains will, of course, not be used in the institutions, Franken. You're wrong there. The doors on the other hand, will have secure locks on them. That's to be expected in order to safeguard the security and safety of the patients."

"Most likely it's to safeguard the peace of mind of Clausdom parents."

"We aim to protect these kids from harm; even to them harming themselves by getting out and about without strict supervision. We'll watch over them more closely than their parents ever did."

"Locks, chains, bodyguards, whatever; you're still sequestering God-fearing children who mean you no harm."

"It's being done for their own good. When you started trying to save every severely deformed child who was born, instead of having a discussion and putting the misfit ones down, you upset the apple cart of Clausdom's perfection paradigm. And doing the same for animals only magnifies imperfections in a perfect society."

Nicholas Henry said, "I was trying to do what was right for all concerned. That's why I started with the animals first, not the children."

"Whatever. Your whole approach has gotten to be too much. I can't believe most citizens want that for Clausdom. I love taking care of animals in need. They don't hold grudges. They aren't mean-spirited. More importantly, I've never known one to stab me in the back simply because things I do things differently."

"I'm going to forgive you for that barb, Brother Franken. I do believe it came out as being a little harsher than was called for; even for you."

"Animals have rights just as much as those handicapped children you're imprisoning."

"What's good for one is good for all."

"I don't know how you can honestly stand there and tell me it's best for all concerned, if we return to a period of cruelty to animals and of inhuman abuse to unsightly children. We've come a long way, Nicholas Henry, since Medieval Clausdom."

"I understand what you are saying. I am not insensitive to your feelings. But maybe this will change over time to more of your liking; once we've gotten control of our breeding standards again, and Christmas quotas are being reached in the workshops. For now at least, it's been decided. What's done is done."

"And you're sure it's final? There's nothing I can do? No recourse to save the status quo?"

"None whatsoever. It's a done deal. I've been ordered to deliver the Twenty-Four Elders' verdict straight to you, face to face; and to answer any questions you might have regarding the outcome. So, do you have any questions? It's getting late."

A Frankenclaus Book!

12
OFF COMES ONE LACE

DOCTOR FRANKEN WENT SILENT, moving two steps sideways to his right and three steps back.

His intention was to get closer to the door; perhaps subconsciously hoping the shorter the distance, the speedier his exit would be from what had in one evening, become a longsuffering day of remembrance for him.

His frown deepened, his eyes softly closed.

The verdict from the Twenty-Four Elders was harsh, but not all that surprising; given it came from men buried in the history of ancestry and traditional rituals.

Franken was hurt not because he hadn't seen similar judgments occur in the past against others; he was hurt because this time the Elders ire was directed towards him and those he loved the most in Clausdom.

He was a Claus, all right; but this time, his being a Claus son wasn't enough to calm the storm being laid against his loved ones.

Inhaling profoundly, he whispered, "I don't know what to say. My boys and girls will at least have roofs over their head; I suppose that's something. Hard telling where my animals will end up; dead, most likely."

"Where your animals end up, dear Brother, the High Court will leave to you. The tundra or Neitherland; those are your choices. You do have the outside option of shipping them down south for food, but I didn't think you would want that. Whatever you decide, they can't stay here."

"I'll choose Neitherland, of course. At least in that region, some of the animals will have a chance to survive. The tundra is certain death."

"I expected as much and told the Elders so. By the way, the Elders figured you'd prefer to assist the dinos in some capacity wherever they went. They'll support you in what you decide. So will I, as Santa Claus."

A light went off in Franken's mind; he thought quickly less the open window of opportunity close on him.

He said, "Unless my animals have some sort of ongoing support to survive, Santa, you're as much as sentencing them to death before the first month is up. It would, of course, be mentioned in the Annals. Are you planning any life support for them at all?"

"The strongest of the lot will survive; somehow, some way, they always do. It's Darwin's Law in domino motion."

"You didn't answer my question, Santa Nick. The animals will need a doctor's close supervision while they're adapting to the new environment. Have you forgotten some of them are crippled with debilitating diseases?"

"I was thinking they could be part of the first batch going to the tundra."

"Why? So they'd be the first to die?"

"Don't look at me like that. You're talking like they're human. Read my lips. They-are-animals, deformed animals at that. Hello? They get what they get. It's no different in Clausdom than it is the world over. It's only been different here because of you and your strange beliefs about animals having rights."

"You're cold, Nicholas; really cold. What about my children's hospital here in Clausdom? What are the Elders planning for it? Do I get to keep it as is, for the patients I have left?"

"The upper floors will be rezoned for normal patients only. Folks will still be bringing their deformed babies to you, same as always; but they'll be received into the basement complex, where there's less foot traffic to see them."

"There's not enough room in the basement for all my patients. That's ridiculous."

"We're expecting you to have fewer patients as time goes by; through attrition enhanced breeding. But if necessary, you can add more patients per room. I know it doesn't sound right; but it is right. It's for the greater good. A few must suffer so the majority can live better lives."

"At least the Elders included Neitherland as an option for my animals," Franken said. "It's funny how I've always told Frankie Anne how the wilderness region over there had potential, should Clausdom proper ever become overpopulated. I had no idea it would be so soon."

"It's only overpopulated with dinos. Everything else will come into balance in Clausdom, once the dinos are gone."

"Now, that's the part I really don't understand. The Twenty-Four Elders are callous; I get that. But you? You're Santa Claus. It's not Christian to separate oneself from those needing help. Yet, you seem to have no problem with it at all. How can this be?"

"It's tradition, Brother Franken. Being Christian has nothing to do with how we treat animals. They have no spirits, remember? They're dimwit dumb."

"They have souls; I know they have souls. On top of which, animals don't sin. They can't. I personally believe I'll see them in Heaven. And I find nothing in the Bible which says I won't." He took a step forward. "What's more, Mister Know-it-All, you can't tell me otherwise."

"Hey, look, don't get huffy on me. I intend to support any efforts to improve Neitherland to receive your animals as best I can. At least in the beginning, I will.

Consider it a Nice gift from a Nice Santa and in hindsight, from the Elders themselves."

"Thank them for me in hindsight then."

FRANKEN JACK had drifted over towards the portrait of Sinterclaus. Once there, he reached down and threw his bag over his right shoulder.

Santa Nicholas said, "Don't jump out the door just yet, Franken. We're not heartless folks. We'll help you with the changeover. Sit back down and hear what we'll do for your animals in the transition. Leaving won't solve anything. Let's talk. You may be surprised at the kindness of the Twenty-Four Elders."

"You talk. I'll listen." He dropped the bag to the floor.

"First, let me tell you what I'll do as Santa. I'll go so far as to promise you Clausdom will help out with survival resources the entire first year the animals are there. That's something, isn't it? What's more, you got my Santa word on it. I'm not cold-blooded on how this is affecting your lifestyle. You're still my brother."

"They need more help than for just one year, Nick, if they're expected to survive on their own."

"One year is all the Elders will let me do; period. They either survive or they don't. Try not to make this more complicated than it already is. I'm trying to be fair. I don't even have to do the year. I'm trying to work with you on this."

Nicholas rose and walked around back of the soft chair where Franken was seated. He retrieved the doughnut tray and held it out to his brother.

"Here; have another doughnut. We might as well finish these off while they're fresh."

"Thanks," Franken said dryly; picking out a small, but shapely Clausdo. He didn't intend to eat this one; just lick the thick stack of frosted flakes off the top. Then he'd put it back on the plate.

After his first lick, he said, "What is the Elders' timetable on having the last of the dinodeer removed? They're the ones I have the most of as being disabled."

"Officially? Ninety days from the end of this next Christmas gift-run; this is four weeks away. Unofficially, yesterday's not soon enough. That being said, I don't intend to do any enforcing of any of the migration in the immediate future. You've got time to plan things out."

As he was answering, Santa Nick set the tray down on the coffee table; within close reach of his brother's long arms as a temptation. He anticipated his brother being more agreeable on a fuller stomach.

"Gee thanks, Santa Claus," Franken said dryly. "You're giving me a whole four weeks and ninety days in which to lay out an all-inclusive survival foundation for an entire culture of handicapped souls."

Santa Nick shook his head. "Christmas Eve is around the corner, Franken. The gift-run comes first; you know that. I'm going to be extremely busy playing catch-up to have all the gifts ready. And I've told the Elders as much. I won't be dealing with the dinos until the New Year."

"So you said."

"When this next gift-run is over, I will formally announce the upcoming changes as part of our New Year's Resolutions for Clausdom."

"Naughty resolutions is what they'll be this year," chipped in Franken.

"They are solutions to issues which will then set the stage for next year's gift workload. The resolutions themselves aren't Naughty or Nice, per se."

"Matter of opinion."

"Just remember, those New Year's resolutions will include the feeding of your dinos in Neitherland for a spell. So don't speak ill of them. By the end of the first quarter's work, the Elders expect all dinodeer to be out of Clausdom."

"That's a fast timetable."

"It is; but like they say, waste not, want not."

"I'll have to begin setting up receiving shelters in Neitherland before winter is over."

"Totally expected. We'll supply the resources for the shelters and such. You have to do the bulk of the work with what dino volunteers you have. I'm not taking any of my shop workers off making next year's gifts, just to build shelters for one-legged animals; can't afford to."

"I'm aware of that. Some of my dinos won't last the winter if I move them too soon. Are you sure you want them on your conscience?"

NICHOLAS CLAUS STOOD and promptly turned his back to his birth marked brother; listening to his next words rebound off the wall.

"Don't make this personal; Franken Jack. It's not what I want or don't want that matters. It's the larger picture, remember? The greater good?" He turned back around.

"Animals are the larger picture in my life. They are my greater good. You're taking that away from me."

"If you weren't a Claus, it'd be different. We wouldn't even be having this conversation. But you are a Claus. Nevertheless, the spirit of Christmas is more important than us caring for deformed animals. If your animals have to be sacrificed so Christmas Eve's gift-run can be saved, so be it."

"It sickens me to hear you talk like that."

"Well, it wouldn't be the first time animals have been sacrificed on a daily basis for the greater good. We wouldn't even have Clausdom if it weren't for Christmas. And we wouldn't even have Christmas if it weren't for the animal sacrifices in Jerusalem. It's why we exist. It's why we have the Twenty-Four Elders."

"Even so, Nicholas Henry, I personally believe God created dinos the way He wanted them to be; to give Him glory in areas where glory was absent. Each of them is just one more way of glorifying God."

"God created them perfect, sure. But something went awry during their time of gestation. So even though God created them perfect in the beginning, they sure didn't come out that way; did they?"

"No. But I don't blame God because of their imperfections. Nor do I blame Him for mine."

"I don't begrudge you loving animals, Brother Franken; just you're putting their welfare before the success of the Christmas gift-run. Now, let's talk specifics on this Neitherland move."

"I'm ready."

"To keep you happy and because you're a Claus son who is of age, the Elders are giving me a long rope to help out. So, if you like, I can place you in full charge of gathering up the dinos and delivering them and what resources are needed to the Neitherland region."

"I'd like that. Make it happen."

"Consider it done. You name it; I'll get it for you. The best part is you can set things up in a manner that best befits the misfits; if you get my drift," Santa Nick smiled at his rank humor.

Doctor Franken only scowled; saying nary a word.

A Frankenclaus Book!

13
OFF COMES THE OTHER!

FRANKEN CLAUS IGNORED the unseemly taunt tossed in his direction about those he cared for who were different in appearance.

With barbs from his childhood having been so traumatic because of his appearance, Franken had become relatively hardened to others trying to either embarrass, or intimidate him with fear and insecurity.

When it came to his own Santa brother now doing it, he preferred to remain meek; which is to say, he chose to have an attitude which allowed others to treat him unfairly.

He said, "It would do me good to oversee the migration personally, Nicholas; thank you. The animals won't be near as agitated at the radical shift in locales. They know I'll take care of them, whatever the surroundings."

"True enough, I suppose. I do know they won't be nearly as jittery if they see a friendly face helping them along; especially one as familiar as yours. They will move along at a faster pace, shortening the time needed for the transition."

"That's precisely what I was thinking."

"Well, Brother Claus," Nicholas said, "great minds think alike. Besides, you helping out will sit well with the gift-shop workers. They'll be glad to know you're working with us in turnkey fashion on this."

"Hold it right there, Nick; let's get one thing clear," Franken said, "I'm doing what I believe is best for the welfare of the animals. That is all. I am not happy with this in the least. I certainly don't agree with what is being done."

"Be that as it may, you've chosen the right side in dealing with our dino-dilemma. That you're willing to help us move them out is a God-send. I'll be broadcasting your leadership role all over Clausdom. It'll make us both look good and I'll be able to provide you with more resources in Neitherland because of it."

"I still have my reservations."

"So do I; on how much help I should give as Santa. But when we're done, the local workers will be making twice the gifts in half the time. Morale will skyrocket. It will also make me look exceptionally competent before the Elders."

"Are we done here, Nicholas? I've plans to design; futures to plan out."

Santa Nick said, "I've only one more thing to mention; then you can be off. But first, let me fill up your cup before the hot chocolate gets cold. We'll toast to our working together as a team."

Nicholas retrieved the chocolate pot.

As his brother stood and held out his cup, Nick filled it to the brim.

As he did so, he casually informed his doctor brother, "By the way, the Elders want a high wall built around your dino orphanages. It'll need to be thick; to make it soundproof."

Pot in hand, Nicholas Henry stood waiting for a reaction. It wasn't long in coming.

His brother was aghast at the idea of using a wall to keep his misfits hidden away; sequestered from those of normal stature.

Doctor Franken declared, "They want to build a wall? They just don't stop, do they? Why on earth would they want a wall built? The orphans aren't going to hurt anyone."

"Two reasons; both for the benefit of the orphans. A wall will keep the enclave of loud, community sounds from disturbing the misfits' peace of mind during the day, as well as limit their confusion over why they're different. They will have a sound mind with which to function."

"And the second reason?"

"The structure also increases their safety. If they fall down or go banging their heads against a wall wildly, someone will find them sooner to remedy the situation. The wall makes it so those on a rampage can only go so far."

"It sounds more like you're closing them off from society altogether."

"Not totally. I told you it's all voluntary. When the dino animal migration to Neitherland is complete, the standalone buildings left in Clausdom will be renovated for human use. The largest ones will house both the mentally and physically handicapped boys and girls now living with their parents."

"How is that going to work, exactly? You're talking about a large-scale, internal effort."

SANTA NICHOLAS set the hot chocolate pot down next to the Clausdo tray.

"Well, on this coming New Year's Day, the Twenty-Four Elders are putting forth a new marketing campaign; a big one. They intend to convince parents to institutionalize any child whose personal deficiencies take up most of the parents' spare time."

"Not wasting any time on this, are they?"

"Elders don't waste time; we do."

"Yeah, right," Franken said with disdain.

Finishing what remained of the hot chocolate in his cup, Franken Jack downed it in one gulp.

Wiping the dregs off his lips, he reached for the pot, filling it anew.

Nicholas held his words until Franken put the pot down. Then he spoke.

"The Elders are offering free pickup and delivery to the institution of the parent's choice. And home visits are open as often as desired. Which, to tell you the truth, I expect the visits themselves will trickle down to occurring mostly on holidays and such. You know the drill; out of sight, out of mind."

Franken said, "It looks like the Elders are trying to free up family time to make the parents more available for the workshops. That's not much of a benefit to the parents. They lose their handicapped children to the system, and have to work harder in the workplace to meet higher quotas for the same pay."

"It's for the greater good, Franken Jack. Besides, the effective gain goes both ways. We're making it possible for normal people to lead normal lives; to actually live healthier, productive lives."

"With their normal children in a normal family."

"Exactly; it's perfect," Santa Nicholas said. "At the same time, they can reach personal fulfillment by being equally industrious in their capacity as gift-shop workers."

"But it all comes at the expense of the special needs children."

"Parents are people, too. They are just as important as the children; more so, even, in

Clausdom. What we're doing makes it so parents can go out in public and not be sidesaddled with a disabled child going along for the ride to embarrass them."

"Loving parents don't consider themselves sidesaddled with problem children, Nick. Disabled boys and girls simply require more attention than healthy ones. The children are loved equally."

"Whatever; some are, most aren't," Nicholas said. "The bottom line is the handicapped kids will be better taken care of in the state-run institutions. They'll be safer physically, and professional caregivers will provide more enhanced therapeutic care than the parents could ever do."

"Better medical care maybe, but nothing can replace the warmth a disabled child feels from the loving arms of a mother or father holding them close at bedtime."

"Parents can still visit. Did I say they couldn't?" Santa Nicholas inflected. "The kids will get their hugs. The good news is the Elders anticipate workshop performance will increase twofold with the move. Shop numbers will be back up to par by the midway mark. We will have successfully overcome the workshop performance issue."

"You think so?"

"Stop being so pessimistic. It can work. It's not like we're having the crippled children pay for the wall, is it?"

"Isn't it? You're driving them into hiding. I'd say that's paying the price quite nicely for safety and security, when it's nothing more than seclusion."

"Teachers and counselors will be provided as needed in the beginning. They will attend to any dino-kids with normal emotional issues. And the overt outlier ones we decide can be better helped by you, will be phased out to Neitherland through attrition."

"Looks like the Elders have all bases covered."

"Pretty much; that's their job. They are the wisest of us, aren't they?"

"I thought their job was to be sensible, not heartless," Franken asked in a mocking tone.

"I see no reason for sarcasm just because the High Court wants to clean up Clausdom. As Santa, the task to see it comes to pass has been passed on to me."

"What if the dino children behind the wall need the Dome's built-in light-rays to help them get better? What then?"

"I didn't say they couldn't go outside. They just have to be kept behind the new walls and make do with what rays make it in. If normal folks can't see them or hear them, they won't mind them being there. Fool proof, hey?"

"I don't know what to say. I'm shocked this is happening in the hometown of the world famous Santa Claus. What are people going to say when it gets out?"

"People are going to say we're making Clausdom great again."

"Forcing good folks to hide out in fear is a far cry from making Clausdom great again, Nicholas."

Santa Nick stood, chewing his thoughts as he chose his words carefully. "These are tough times, Brother. Tough times require a tough Santa at the helm."

"And that's you?"

"It is for this generation. The world is maturing. Sad as it seems, there's just no room for misfits being seen in public anymore. What's best for them is specialized care in an environment where only their peers see them. It's better for us. It's better for them."

"Well, Nicholas, it's been my experience people make room for those they consider important. I consider all dinos important. That's why I've always shared everything I have with them."

"I know that."

"I still don't understand why the Elders went full throttle on this without involving me. Why didn't I get a chance to object? To speak my piece in defense of the dinos?"

"You just did, Franken," Nicholas walked to the back of the sofa as he spoke; carefully putting the long sofa between him and his brother. "That's what this whole conversation has been about. Everything you've said will go on the record; I guarantee it."

"From your mouth to the Elders' ears, I take it," Franken Claus slurred out derogatorily.

"Something like that. I know it doesn't sound right, but let me reiterate; it's for the greater good. We're all small parts to a big wheel."

"Nick? You're my brother. How do you expect me to react to all this? Peaceably? To just accept it as gospel and let sleeping dogs lie?"

"I expect you to react as a Claus. Nothing that's yours has been destroyed."

"How so?"

"Well, you want to work with the deformed dinodeer? Fine; they'll be in Neitherland and you've free sleigh transportation to get you there and back as often as you want. And you can use the Claus Anointing in doing so. It'll make the trip that much faster."

Franken Jack said, "Neitherland is hours away from Clausdom for everyone else. They don't have the same Anointing we have as Claus sons."

"Parents can visit their children in Neitherland once a month if need be. There will only be a handful there anyway."

"For now."

"For always, hopefully. You want to tend to dinomarked children with deformed bones and missing limbs here in Clausdom? Fine; they'll be in institutionalized orphanages, where they can be looked after by certified professionals on a daily basis."

"All I've worked for my whole life is changing."

"It's changing for the better. You're not losing anything, Franken. You will still have your special needs medical practice and your very precious veterinary service. It's all there for you to oversee. Nothing is being taken away from you."

"It will be different than the way I set up."

"It's just rearranged, is all. The pieces are all still there. Don't sound so down in the dumps. The Elders are simply weeding out the tares and bringing in the sheaves. You'll thank us for this later on. It's for your own good; trust me. Don't you ever get tired of wiping up after these creatures?"

Franken shook his head as he headed for the door.

"That does it. I've had about all of this Santa kindness I can take."

"Don't bite the hand that feeds you, Franken," Nick snapped at his brother's back. "It ain't healthy."

TURNING AROUND, Franken vented to the outside, what he was feeling on the inside.

"I've made my decision. I'll take charge of the dinodeer going to Neitherland, as I've told you. And you'll provide that first year of support like you promised. But I've decided when the last dino is escorted out of

Clausdom, I'll be right behind him; riding drag."

"What's that supposed to mean? What will you be dragging?"

"My own carcass out of Clausdom. It means if you're throwing out the dinodeer, you're throwing me out as well." He downed what dregs remained in his cup with a grunt, and set the cup down hard; next to the pot.

Nicholas Henry reacted with a highly perplexed look on his face.

This was something he hadn't expected.

And neither had the Elders, he imagined.

His brother was leaving?

The Elders would blame him for not keeping his brother's mood swings under control.

And how would he defend himself from twenty-four sharpened tongues?

"You can't be serious, Franken? That's idiotic. Have these dinos gone to your head that much? The Elders never intended to drive you out of Clausdom. You can't go. You're a Claus. You belong in Clausdom."

"I said I'll be going with my dinos. And you and those Elders can take that to the Polar Bank."

"Don't be stupid. You can't survive without a Dome at the North Pole."

"I'll build one."

"With what? Snow and ice and good looks? Forget it. You can't do it alone."

"Then help me find a way, Nick. You said you'd help out the first year. Do it for a longer period of time. Help me out here. I'm your brother. Don't make me do this on my own."

"But what about the disabled orphans? Who will take care of them if you leave? Certainly not me. The regular doctors won't be much help. Making house calls would interrupt their polar games."

"Any that want to come to Neitherland with me, I'll be more than happy to take care of over there. You can double the size of my orphanage, all right; only it'll be in Neitherland."

"Are you in your right mind?"

"I am. And my dino orphanage in Neitherland won't have any walls around it. Any parents, who don't want to take care of their special needs children, can send them to me there. I'll be more than happy to take care of them along with the orphans."

"You'd do that? You'd choose them uncomely creatures over us? Over Clausdom? Over Christmas?"

"If my animals go, I go."

"What? That's absurd!"

"If they have to pay a price for being different, I should pay the same price for being just as different. Are you sure you still want to go through with this, Nick? Remember what I said; this will all go in the Annals of Clausdom."

"Because you are a Claus son?"

"Because I am a Claus son."

Nicholas said, "Well, Claus son or not, I have no choice. The Elders are driving this, not me. I'm just the messenger."

"A price will be paid on both sides of the aisle, Nicholas Henry. Clausdom will lose its second Claus son; first Bourbon and now me. And the particulars of this will go in the yearly Annals under your watch. History will most likely say you should have done better on my behalf."

"Hold your tongue, Mister. It's not me holding the reins in this. I've been given an absolute directive that's already been approved by consensus of the Twenty-Four Elders. I have to uphold what they've decreed or I cease being Santa. Christmas would take a hit because there's no one else to do it but you, and you're leaving."

"Moving my animals to the tundra or Neitherland was at your suggestion, was it not? And the Elders having a discussion on me and my dinos was your idea in the first place, right? I know you've never liked me working with those who have disabilities from the beginning."

"It's not you and it's not them. It's Christmas. Christmas comes first. To be honest, Franken, more is expected from a Claus than constantly working with deformed dinos. A visit on occasion is okay, but you've gone way overboard on it. To devote your life to their kind is silly."

"Not for me, it isn't."

"And to answer your question, I went to the Elders when I was inundated with complaints. I'll admit that much. But I never intended on it affecting you to the extent you're making it. You're blowing this all out of proportion."

"I just wish I had had more of a say in the matter before the edict was handed down. I didn't, though. So, I guess that's it. We're done here, Nicholas. Frankie Anne is waiting on me."

"I guess we are done. Give Frankie my regards. If you change your mind on this, let me know. I'll work with you if you stay, or if you go. But I'd much prefer you to stay. You belong here."

"There's nothing more to talk about that I can see. I'd best go pack my bags and start making plans."

A Frankenclaus Book!

14
Uh Oh Failure Now What?

HIS DECISION made, Doctor Franken returned to the east wall to recoup his duffle bag, where he had dropped it earlier.

Nicholas said, "I'm sorry it had to go this way, Franken. I'm against you going. I'll state that flat out. But you'll be back. I doubt you stay there, once you see how poor it is compared to Clausdom. We all have our comfort zone."

"Duly noted and totally wrong," his brother curtly replied. He slung the retrieved bag over his shoulder.

Taking a deep breath, Santa Nicholas Henry Claus threw up his hands into the air. "Fine-Fine-Fine! Now just hold on a minute,

Franken Henry. Let me think on this a minute."

Santa Nicholas had to do something to protect himself and his Santa image from the fallout of his brother's decision. The Elders would have a fit and no doubt, blame him.

Nicholas said, "I don't know why you keep trying to rush out when we haven't reached closure on this. If you're going to be so stubborn as to leave Clausdom, the least I can do is to help as best I can."

"Help is good, Nick. Help is appreciated. And it would be a wise move. It will read well in the Clausdom Annals for both you and the Twenty-Four Elders."

"It had better. The way I see it, the best thing I can do is to make the process go smoother for your move. I'll let everyone know you're moving to Neitherland with the full blessing of the official Santa Claus."

Franken returned his duffle bag to the floor a second time. "You'd do that? You'd give me the official Santa Claus blessing?"

"I would."

"An official blessing would open a number of doors for me," Franken said, taking a step towards his Santa brother. "Thank you. I don't know quite what to say."

"Say nothing. Consider it a gift from Santa Claus. We are family, are we not? It's what family does for its own. What's more, I'll even go so far as to build you a small Dome under which you can live."

"A Dome? Oh, Nicholas, thank you; it's more than I could ever hope for."

"That'll keep you alive at least. It's the least we can do for a member of the Claus Clan. And maybe you can find yourself a good woman and have a Claus son before it's too late. It'll help us out here."

"A Neitherland Dome sounds wonderful. Now, that is what I call helping a brother out, Santa Nick. I owe you one."

"Yes, you do. Now, I can't guarantee the Dome we build will be big enough to house every single one of your dinos in their own private rooms, but we can make it so it'll take the bulk of them and make them comfortable. You can work out the details with Administrator Clarence."

"We'll manage, Nicholas. Your Santa blessing means a great deal to me. I hope it doesn't get you into trouble with the Elders."

"I'll handle that part of things when and if the time comes. As you know, once a Santa blessing is given, it can't be revoked; even by the High Court. To do so, would be an abomination."

Franken Jack said, "You could mention how it will look better for them in this year's History Annals."

"I will do that. And Franken? You need to understand some folks will be hurt by your choosing Neitherland over Clausdom. They'll be more Frankenstein talk."

"I know; I know. Frankenstein talk is something I can live with. My animals now, I can't live without."

"The thing is, Brother, I don't know how much affect you having Santa's blessing will have on the naysayers. They'll be offended."

Nicholas Henry then sat down.

"No different than now, in my opinion."

"What I'm trying to say is you shouldn't get your hopes up on them volunteering to help with the transition. What happens; happens. I'll back your play to the hilt, though. You got my Santa word on it."

"Whatever support I get from the Red House will be appreciated. You've been to Neitherland. You know what we're heading into as well as I do," Franken said, sitting down opposite his Santa brother anew.

"I do know," Nicholas said, reaching over and placing his hand on his brother's knee. "That's why I think you may change your mind. Look, Franken, I can't say I like this idea of you leaving Clausdom."

"It's not my first choice either. But like I said; if my animals go, I go."

Franken moved to the center of the room.

Nicholas said, "Well, if it has to be, it has to be. So be it. I can't do much now, but after the Christmas Eve gift-run, tell you what I'll do. I'll go ahead and free up as many workers as I can to help you for the first thirty days of the New Year."

"Excellent."

"They can collect enough needed modular resources to build a modest Dome and a small hospital to boot. You can have a dinodeer healing up in one room whilst a dino-cripple is recuperating in the next."

Franken felt good. "A novel idea, Nick; it might work; a combination hospital and veterinary clinic. The basics to survive are what is needed in the beginning. You're giving me that. I'd like to start with half-adozen of the largest generators on hand. If you can spare them, that is."

"Large generators are what I'd start with if it were me. I'll release Administrator Clarence and Admin Melvin to discuss the particulars with you. The two of them have their own skill sets. They can consult with you on what is needed for the initial move. From there on in, we'll play it by ear."

"It would be nice if you would send either Clarence or Melvin to Neitherland with me permanently. I could use an experienced administrator to help us set up a method to generate our own electrical grid apart from the portable generators."

"Ho, ho, ho," Santa Nick laughed. "No way is that going to happen, old friend. Those two admins are too important to Christmas in Clausdom to let them go. You can raise up your own admins; though I will allow our two admins to train them."

"I had to ask, Nicholas," Franken grinned widely.

"The move to Neitherland will be set up as the Priority One, First-Quarter Project for Clausdom. We'll run an assembly line making walls and rafters. I may even ask the High Court for a spring extension on their first quarter deadline if we feel it's necessary."

"That would be appreciated."

"It would allow the straggler dinos to stay in Clausdom till late spring. They'd have a better chance at surviving the migration then. I'd like this done right, for the Annals sake."

"Thank you, Santa Nick. Again, it means a lot to me to have your Santa blessing."

"It's yours, Brother; though, I'll beat a dead deer one last time. I'd much rather you remain here in Clausdom. But if that can't happen at this point in time, I'm willing to roll the dice and rope-a-dope against the punches. May God go with you when the smoke clears."

FRANKEN STOOD and shook the wrinkles out of his loose trousers. He had won one round and lost one round. But his handicapped animals had been saved.

"Well, this has sure been an interesting day," he said. "I'd best go. Those migration plans aren't going to make themselves and Frankie probably thinks I've fallen off a cliff."

Nick walked to the double doors to see his brother off. "Enjoy making them plans, Franken Jack. You know where to find me when you need me. And I'll be sure to send word to Clarence and Melvin on this. I'll make sure they back you all the way behind the scenes."

Santa Nicholas Claus watched as his brother, bag in hand, exited through the large doors without looking back.

Nicholas was thankful the whole, sorry ordeal was over. It wasn't what he wanted; but the Twenty-Four Elders would get what they wanted, and his blood brother would save his animals.

Now, as Santa, it was left up to him to make it all come to pass without too many red flags muddying the snows of Clausdom.

The Elders would be both pleased and unhappy at his performance as Santa. Yet, he'd done what he could at the time, to protect what was going to be said about the Elders in the Clausdom Annals, concerning one Franken Jack Claus and his departure from Clausdom.

All Twenty-Four Elders would just have to understand, how the modifications their duly appointed Santa Claus had made to the

High Court's migration plans was for them and him; to protect their image being handed down to future generations as an honorable one when it came to the Claus heritage.

It was now passed his dinnertime; reminded as he was by the sound of his growling stomach crying out for food.

Nicholas knew he'd have to settle for leftovers, as his wife had no doubt already retired for the evening.

As that thought took root, Nick glanced towards the Clausdo tray. There was one left; a small one.

A Frankenclaus Book!

15
PICKING UP PIECES
MOVING ON

IN THE KINGDOM OF CLAUSDOM, time passed quickly for the two Claus sons.

Christmas quotas were reached through longer hours and fewer breaks, duplicating everyone's efforts of the previous December month.

Nicholas had been right about the reaction of the Twenty-Four Elders to Franken Claus' departure, and to their Santa backing the move with the official Santa blessing.

Nevertheless, the Elders confessed, the actions on their part would be so written in the Annals of Clausdom, to reflect the High

213

Court's willing efforts to appease all sides fairly.

THE NEITHERLAND MIGRATION PROJECT surrounding Doctor Franken's dinos reached completion in the spring.

In an effort of good will, the Elders had relented on the strictness of the ninety-day exit notice. Once started, project deadline requirements mushroomed quite rapidly and unexpected adjustments were made.

By the time summer had arrived, the Neitherland Dome was ready for occupancy. The skeletal foundation for Neitherland proper had not only been well-defined, but was seen to be thriving quite well in the works being done on its behalf.

The last of the dino animals were migrated out of Clausdom; a notable accomplishment for all.

Nicholas and Franken had said their goodbyes as brothers; even as friends who had worked side by side to create a survivable environment for Doctor Franken, his daughter and their animals, in the third region of the North Pole.

There at the last, Franken Jack informed Santa Nicholas how from that day forth, his

Claus name would be appended to his first name; albeit, Frankenclaus.

Doctor Franken was changing it in honor of the brave animals and orphans who had faith in a Claus son to take a chance at wilderness living. Changing the name was him identifying with them and the changes they were making to survive.

Doctor Frankenclaus, it was; Nicholas Henry surmised. He was none too happy with it, but there was nothing he could do. What was a space between names? Nothing; literally.

There was no Clausdom edict which declared 'A man shall not change his name,' or 'A Claus son will always keep his Claus surname.'

Thus, from that day forward, the name of Doctor Frankenclaus was written in stone; and by stone, that is to say it was scribed so in the History Annals of Clausdom, with a clear hand and a firm edit as to why it had been allowed.

As promised, Nicholas Henry as the reigning Santa used his authoritative position to officially proclaim his ongoing Santa blessing over the new crowned House of Frankenclaus in Neitherland.

To that extent, after all was said and done, considerable resources continued to be sent to Neitherland from Clausdom proper in the subsequent months; more than enough to complete the planned building projects for not just the first year as promised, but for the first two years.

Per the High Court's stipulation, the Clausdom History Annals would so note the kind-hearted generosity of the Twenty-Four Elders on behalf of a male, Claus descendent.

A compact two-story hospital was constructed, along with scores of highly efficient, cookie-cutter, modular track homes.

The migration process had been a success all the way around.

And it was so written in Clausdom's History Annals; which gave most of the credit to the Twenty-Four Elders of Clausdom and the Santa Claus they set in charge of it all.

THE NEW CULTURE in Neitherland flourished from a seed; ultimately becoming more self-sustaining over time.

As it grew, ongoing support from Clausdom receded into the background as planned. After three years, it had ceased altogether.

When Neitherland's animal hospital came online, an outstanding order was issued in Clausdom. This order decreed all newborn dinodeer in Clausdom were to be automatically escorted to the Neitherland Hospital within seven days of birth.

It did not come as a surprise to anyone. All knew by the time the edict came out, how Doctor Franken had taken up permanent residence in Neitherland. Being there, he was also more than ready to receive the newborn deer that were abnormal in some way.

In the succeeding years since the full completion of the dino migration, little communication had passed between the two regions.

The automated process of migrating dino animals out of Clausdom continued without fail, however; with dinos being happily sent and summarily received as decreed.

Over time, a steady stream of Clausdom parents sent their dino-elves to Neitherland as well.

It was no secret Doctor Frankenclaus was the only doctor dedicated to enriching the restricted lives of physically disabled and badly disfigured boys and girls.

Thus, the move was not only prudent on the part of the parents, but preferential for the welfare of their special needs children.

In Neitherland, the dino children and dinomarked animals found ready acceptance as being normal. Their overabundance of disabilities and malformations became naught but a platform of vibrant potential for future growth in Neitherland society.

No longer were they gazed upon as freaks of nature in God's perfect Clausdom world.

In their new home, they were just one of many dinos; free to expand their roles in society while at the same time, lending a helping hand to others with like disabilities, without fear of humiliation and closet condemnation.

Santa Nicholas Claus recalled how he'd coined the nickname, frankenjack, for his brother's favorites; the dinodeer cast-offs which were methodically migrated to Neitherland.

Nicholas had nicknamed the animals after his brother; partly out of endearment; partly out of him realizing how much he would miss the company of his older brother; who had proved himself obsessively dedicated to saving such handicapped creatures.

Some of Santa Nick's more selfish worker elves, however, seemed agitated at the migration. They helped without complaint, of course; but rumor control already had it they were very comfortable in calling the Neitherland Veterinarian by a new name; one Doctor Frankenclaus, the Creator of New Life in the Neitherland Wilderness.

But when they heard their reigning Santa Claus use the same term in public more than once, they assumed his using it was done by Elder approval; thus, clearing their using it as often as they wanted.

Thinking back on it, Nicholas realized he'd been wrong in using Franken's new name to make fun of him and his patients during the migration; like some of the workshop elves now did as a matter of record.

It was wrong of him, and he would have to correct its use over time, in Clausdom.

Santa Nicholas came to realize the taking on of new names was symbolic of a new era of living at the North Pole; one created by a Claus son.

His brother had a new name, his dinodeer now had a new name and others were being given new names; names they could answer to without shame.

Thus, there was new life in Neitherland for all; led by a Claus son of the House of Claus in the Kingdom of Clausdom.

Disfigured children were referred to under the singular umbrella name of dinomark.

In a sense, Santa Nicholas knew, they too had been named after his brother; but not by him; for they were indeed, marked. And they were far from being perfect.

It wasn't long before the citizens of Clausdom followed their Santa's lead of inventing new names and expressions for Doctor Frankenclaus' special needs obsession. The good citizens ended up adopting these same colloquial expressions they made up in their own, everyday speech.

To Santa Nick's way of thinking, what had happened between him and his brother was fate; a form of Claus destiny over which he had little say and less control.

It was kind of like the birthmark on Franken's face.

Who could control the formation, much less the appearance of a birthmark?

No one could.

If it was there at birth, it was there at death.

That being the case, Santa Nick took it by faith all had turned out for the best.

He was Santa and Franken with his now-changed name to Frankenclaus, had his own Kingdom of Neitherland; over which he had total control.

There was, however, one unspoken part of Santa Nick's flesh which rubbed him raw down deep.

It had been hard for him to live down the personal shame of how his own flesh and blood had rejected Clausdom and Christmas, for a bunch of dino-marred creatures of little value to proper society.

As the Clausdom Santa, Nicholas Henry believed Christmas gift-giving was the highest priority of concern for a Claus-born son; even if half a person's face happened to be purplish red.

Santa Nicholas understood how higher standards needed to be observed by those of higher calling.

The Elders even spoke of it with the edicts they put forth.

The full story of the outcome of the migration could only be seen in hindsight. Its future was yet to come; which, of course, brings us to transporting ourselves from Book-1 into Book-2 of The *Frankenclaus* Christmas for Santa Claus Book Series.

*Note: If you have thoughts of constructive points of interest concerning this Book, please put them in the Amazon Review when you submit it.

Make it short and to the point...thx.

For US reviews, go to the following:

http://www.amazon.com/dp/B08GJR6HFB

UPCOMING BOOK-2:
Santa Lost In Polar Triangle!

A shortage of Claus sons becomes a major problem for the Twenty-Four Elders of the High Court of Clausdom; when Santa Nicholas Claus fails to return to Clausdom on Christmas morning.

The hunt ensues, but the frigid search can only be done on land; as only a Claus with the Claus Anointing can fly using reindeer driven sleighs.

The names of Frankenclaus and Bourbon Claus come up, but there are reservations on calling on either of these twins to assist,

It is well-known both are jealous the Twenty-Four Elders of Clausdom chose their younger brother to be the reigning Santa; over them.

A Frankenclaus Book!

!

Why I Wrote This Book

I WROTE THIS BOOK BECAUSE I love the celebration of Christmas each and every year.

Not the gifts so much; it was because it forced people to consider the plight of others relative to their own; and to help if they could.

When I was growing up, this month of December brought more joy to my life than any other month.

I don't know if it was because it forced my father to be nice, or if I was encouraged by all wanting to participate.

I do know it taught us kids to remember it was more blessed to give and forgive, than it was to harbor ill will against one another.

What better heavenly Christmas could any of us possibly wish for, than to be forgiven by those we have hurt?

Santa God is good.../FFF

See you in Frankenclaus Book-2 Santa Claus Lost in the Polar Triangle!

Dear Reader,

This concludes Book-1 of A Frankenclaus Christmas for Santa Claus.

Following is a Glossary of New Words you will come across throughout this multi-book series of Frankenclaus Presents.

See you in Book-2.

I will try to have the entire series out by Christmas morning, when Santa returns to Clausdom~!

For all other country reviews, see below:
1. Go to www.amazon.com
2. Search for this Book Title: "A Frankenclaus Christmas"
3. Scroll down three (3) pages
4. Locate Customer Reviews
5. Click on 'Write a Customer Review.'

Glossary of New Words

BLAST YOU: an expression of intense disgust

BP: acronym for big person; slang; specifically denoting a person more than four feet nine inches.

CLAUS ANOINTING: The Anointing peculiar to Claus siblings; genetically handed down from generation to generation. It allows the recipient to enter into hyper-mode when it comes to movement of arms and legs of a Claus sibling's body.

CLAUS-DOME: An adjustable, cylindrical cover overshadowing Clausdom proper; protecting it from the harsh elements of living at the North Pole.

CLAUSDOM: One of three inhabitable regions at the North Pole; home to Nicholas Henry Claus.

DEER-GONE-IT: an expression representing frustrating and generally used in reference to one's own lackluster efforts.

DINO: A dino is any person or animal who is handicapped or blemished; denotes one who lacks perfection in one or more areas of life.

DINOASHIT: an expression which denotes the act of permanently removing objects or items from one's sight and presence; returns substance to ashes from whence it came.

DINODEER: An imperfect deer; tarnished or flawed in some unsightly manner.

DINODIRT: slang for associating one's predicament with a dino's waste; used to describe the excrement of disfigured animals or handicapped elves.

DINODOG: A flawed dog in need of a missing limb.

DINODRAT: A term of frustration in the highest degree.

DINODUFAS: A slang term expressing displeasure at someone's lack of understanding of real-time events.

DINOGOAT: Carefully selected animals used by Bourbon for his Naughtiest of the Naughty sleigh.

DINOMARK: A blemished animal of any species.

DINODUMP: The act of solid waste management; the act of doing number two.

DINODUNG: Poop; excretion in one form or another, coming from a handicapped dino.

DINOSTUPID: the immediate resultant act of doing something foolish after just having been told not to do it.

DINOWHIZ: the act of liquid waste management; the act of doing number one.

DMAIC: Method to troubleshoot problems: Define, Measure, Analyze, Improve, Control. A strategy intended to optimize efficiency in project processes, while minimizing mistakes and errors in judgment using widely collected, data-driven statistics.

DWARF: A person of short stature, generally under 4' 9".

ELDERDAMIT: an expression used to describe feelings rising out of one's own failed efforts. This term is a weak attempt to impose a higher power's judgment into play, targeting obstacles which overpower us and put us to shame.

FRANKENJACK: Term referencing all reindeer in Neitherland; dino and normal.

FRANKIT: An expression used by Clausdom residents as a derogatory slang term expressing one's frustration; coming about after Franken Jack Claus forsook the Christmas of Clausdom in favor of saving disabled dinos.

GOLDEN CIRCLE: A circle of streaming rays which penetrates Earth's geomagnetic core.

HAILSTORMS: An expression comparing one's thoughts to virtual weather conditions.

LP: acronym for little person; slang; specifically denoting a person less than four foot nine inches.

MIDGET: An offensive term – labeling persons of short stature as being less than what they are.

NEITHERLAND: One of three inhabitable regions at the North Pole; home to Franken Jack Claus.

SNOWBALLS AND HAILSTONES: Slang terms denoting frustration; to be caught betwixt a snowball and a hailstone when making a decision.

SNOWBALLS ON FUR TAILS: An offhand expression denoting irritation brought on by either mild or extreme disappointment.

SNOWBLAST: A slang expression used to denote extreme anger and disappointment; snowblast it!

SNOWHOUND: slang for a penguin which refuses to follow the leader during migratory marches.

SANTA ANOINTING: The Anointing bestowed upon the designated Claus sibling; who has been selected by the High Court of Clausdom to be the reigning Santa Claus for the current generation of God's children. It gives the recipient a plethora of mystical powers; all of which are used to deliver gifts to boys and girls the world over; all in one night's timeframe.

SUPER SANTA ANOINTING: The Super Santa Anointing is only given out during times of disaster. It is administered by the laying on of hands of the Twenty-Four Elders of Clausdom, and is only given to the reigning Santa Claus in an emergency. The combined twenty-four fold Anointing gives super-duper powers to Santa; such as the power to create fire out of thin air and the power to move heavy objects about at will. It also gives the reigning Santa the power to heal to the point of raising one from the dead by the laying on of hands, and allowing the Anointing to flow whilst driving sickness from the body. Once given, this gift is irrevocable.

TOR: One of three inhabitable regions at the North Pole; home to Bourbon Tor Claus.

TORRID: a citizen of the Tor region who had sworn allegiance to Bourbon Tor Claus.

TP: acronym for tall person; slang; specifically denoting a person more than four feet nine inches.

A Frankenclaus Christmas for Santa Claus

233